Rights and Respect

and RIGHTS RESPECT

What You Need to Know About Gender Bias and Sexual Harassment

by Kathlyn Gay

The Millbrook Press Brookfield, Connecticut

Library of Congress Cataloging-in-Publication Data
Gay, Kathlyn.
Rights and respect: what you need to know about
gender bias and sexual harassment / by Kathlyn Gay.
p. cm.
Includes bibliographical references (p.   ) and index.
Summary: Describes sexual harassment in school and
at work, explains the relationship of harassment to sex
discrimination, and explores methods of preventing
gender bias and harassment.
ISBN 1-56294-493-2 (lib. bdg.)
1. Sexual harassment of women—United States—
Juvenile literature. 2. Sexual harassment in
education—United States—Juvenile literature.
[1. Sexual harassment.] I. Title.
HQ1237.5.U6G39   1995
305.42´0973—dc20   94-45501   CIP   AC

Published by The Millbrook Press Inc.
2 Old New Milford Road, Brookfield, Connecticut 06804

I am indebted to
Karen and Dean Hamilton and Nissa Gay
for their help with research.
Thank you all.

I deeply appreciate the help provided by
Ellen Krulewitch, who has worked on
discrimination cases as the Civil Rights
Director for the city of Elkhart, Indiana,
and who used her legal training to explain
the law regarding sex discrimination and
sexual harassment.

A special thanks also to the individuals
who shared their experiences with me but
who wish to remain anonymous.

KATHLYN GAY

Contents

Rights and Respect

CHAPTER ONE

What Is Sexual Harassment?

FRANCES CONLEY, M.D.
a neurosurgeon

LIEUTENANT PAULA COUGHLIN
a naval officer

TERESA HARRIS
a former salesperson for a forklift company

ANITA HILL
a law professor

CHELTZIE HENTZ
a student

This short list is representative of the women and girls who have publicly related the traumas they've experienced because of sexual harassment. Those who are harassed come from all walks of life and range from elementary-school students to women over fifty. The list grows longer daily, but only a relatively small number of victims speak or write openly about their experiences because it is a risky matter—emotionally, socially, and often financially—to accuse someone who harasses. Frequently women and girls who make complaints about sexual harassment are not believed or are ignored or labeled as "troublemakers."

Men and boys also have been subjected to sexual harassment. A few widely publicized incidents and a popular novel, *Disclosure* by Michael Crichton (it tells the tale of a female boss who harasses a male subordinate), give the impression that an increasing number of women are harassing men. But that is not the case. Surveys, statistics, and court cases show that men and boys are usually the initiators of harassing behavior and direct it primarily at women and girls.

According to the federal Equal Employment Opportunity Commission (EEOC), men filed only 968 of the 10,577 sexual harassment complaints made in 1992.[1] A review of both scientific and nonscientific literature on sexual harassment published in the *American Journal of Psychiatry* in January 1994 found that sexual harassment affected 42 percent of women and 15 percent of men in the workplace. A much larger percentage—73 percent—of women in medical school were harassed, while 22 percent of the men in medical training reported being harassed.[2]

Increasing reports of sexual harassment indicate that the problem is more common than most people realized just a few years ago, and the reported incidents underscore the larger issue—sex discrimination (discrimination based on gender) against women and girls. While federal and state laws against sex discrimination and sexual harassment cover *only* the workplace and educational institutions and job- or school-sponsored events, some women and girls have become more vocal about sexually motivated aggravation on the street and in other public places. Unless someone is physically assaulted, however, there is no legal recourse for street harassment, such as wolf calls and sexual comments. But even if sexually motivated conduct is not deemed illegal, it can adversely affect the person who is the target.

Patty's Story

Over the years, countless women have been the targets of unwanted (and now *illegal*) sexual attention—verbal or physical or both—in the workplace. Sometimes that attention seems to be simply friendly joking and "fooling around," as Patty, a graduate student in sociology at Notre Dame University in northern Indiana, described it. For Patty, the workplace harassment "began so subtly that I really didn't know what was happening until it was far too late," she said.[3]

Patty was a teenager at the time, working in a restaurant in a summer tourist town. She knew the head chef and part owner of the restaurant, a man she called Mark (not his real name), who was married and like a "trusted family friend." But, as Patty reported, Mark started to ask numerous questions about her sexuality: Whom did she date? What qualities did she like in men? Was she a virgin? Would she consider sleeping with him?

"I thought he was joking," Patty said. She told Mark that since he was a married man she couldn't sleep with him, and she tried "not to insult him because he was my boss and—I thought—my friend." But then as time went on, Mark's questioning became "more direct and insistent," and he found ways to touch.

"The first time . . . I was sitting in a chair, waiting for the restaurant to open. Mark came up to me and grazed my leg with his hand. He said he wanted to know if I had shaved my legs that day. I remember feeling startled and just weird about it, but again I shrugged it off as just another form of jest."

Patty related that at other times Mark would get close enough to brush his hand or body across her breasts. Once more she excused the behavior—it was probably accidental, she remembered thinking. But one night after the restaurant had closed and the cleanup crew was at work with music blasting, Mark caught Patty alone in an area where she was cleaning tables.

> He backed me into a corner and pushed his body against mine. It was dark and I screamed. He laughed and joked and said all he wanted was to kiss me, and if he could kiss me, he'd back off. I can still feel his body against mine, I can see his face, I can smell the kitchen on him. I let him kiss my cheek, and he finally backed off. All the while I could hear the music in the kitchen, wondering if they would ever hear me screaming.

The harassment did not end with the forced kiss. Not long afterward, she was assaulted while at work in the restaurant kitchen. "Mark grabbed me between my legs. . . . Of course, he made sure no one saw what had happened. I went to slap him, and he caught my hand and laughed. I felt so humiliated."

Patty finally told another employee in the restaurant about the situation. "My friend was appalled. . . .

She told the other owner of the restaurant what had happened. I was ready to quit, but the other owner asked me to stay and said he would talk to Mark."

Although Mark no longer harassed Patty after that, he continued the same type of behavior with another girl, who apparently welcomed the attention. (Welcome sexual overtures are not illegal sexual harassment by today's laws.) When Patty pointed out the behavior, Mark made her life "a living hell," forcing her to quit her job with good pay and leave friends with whom she enjoyed working.

Today, Patty said, she often wonders why she did not see the situation clearly from the beginning. But, she said, "I am a shy person . . . and the attention was almost exciting. It sickens me sometimes now that I felt that way."

Patty went on to explain that, like many teenagers, she trusted this older man, who often did "kind things" such as preparing special dinners for her, socializing with her friends after work, and talking to her seriously about her future and schooling. "It was confusing that someone who I considered to be like family, who I had trusted so much, could possibly be doing bad things." Yet Patty said she learned a lot, and her sexual harassment experience prompted her to channel her academic studies toward finding legal solutions for not only sexual harassment but also other offenses against women.

Other Instances of Sexual Harassment

Incidents of sexual harassment on college campuses and in high school and junior high school—and even in elementary school—have been a growing area of concern. Illegal sexual conduct reported in schools includes unwanted touching, grabbing, and pinching and unwelcome verbal harassment as well as physical assaults. But there has been a great deal of controversy over the topic of sexual harassment in schools, partly because, as Patty pointed out, many young people are confused and ambivalent about their sexual feelings. Or they may feel threatened and unsure about what action to take, as was the case in an incident described in a 1993 feature story for a St. Charles, Illinois, high school newspaper:

> A girl we will call Carrie walks into the teacher's office, sits down, and begins to concentrate on her makeup test. It's a cramped room and two other male teachers are talking and laughing at a desk. They start to ask her questions, like "Oh, what a pretty little thing you are—do you need help on your test?" One teacher puts his arm around Carrie, squeezes her. . . . "Teachers aren't supposed to do this," Carrie tells herself . . . but she tries still to ignore her inner voice and pay attention to her test.
> "I felt creepy and really uncomfortable. It made me angry, but I didn't do anything about it. . . . [I] didn't know what to do while it was happening, or how the school would handle it," said Carrie.[4]

Students may also be uncertain whether sexual behavior is truly harassment or flirting and teasing. In some cases, what is labeled unwelcome by one person may be welcomed by another. For example, some students who are targets of sexual comments and jokes or physical sexual behavior (such as butt-pinching and grabbing) consider these laughing matters. But others may find these actions intolerable.

In some instances, students are able to simply say, "Stop it!" and end behavior that they will not tolerate. On the other hand, there are many young people who do not have the self-confidence to speak out. As one woman now out of school recalled: "There was this guy in eighth grade who terrified me, constantly calling me 'big-butt' and chasing me home. My mother told me to ignore him and he'd quit. But he didn't, and I resorted to racing out of school before that jerk could find me. I hate him to this day because I was powerless to stop him."

Such a reaction is common among those who have been sexually harassed but could not label or stop the harassment. And until recently it was commonplace for females in all age groups to hesitate or refuse to do anything about sexual harassment because they felt powerless.

Harassment of Males

Men, too, may feel they are unable to fight back if they are harassed, even though the reaction or experience is not as common as it is for women. In one instance of male harassment, a woman working in a city parks-department office consistently broadcast her sexual exploits to whoever would listen, but she targeted a male coworker for most of her comments. She thought it was funny to sit on his lap and simulate a sexual act. When someone in the office suggested that her behavior was making the man very uncomfortable, she flippantly said, "Oh, he doesn't care. He's gay!" The male worker did not make a formal complaint, because he feared he would be widely ridiculed or would lose his job.

Wendy Reid Crisp, director of the National Association for Female Executives, frequently tells a story about herself to show how women in power positions can harass. The incident occurred when she was editor in chief of a magazine with only two men on the staff, one her boss and the other a subordinate. According to Crisp's story, the male subordinate was walking down the hall, and Crisp commented that she could see the young man's underwear through his khaki pants, exclaiming, "Hey everybody . . . look how cute his buns are." Another woman warned Crisp that she was embarrassing the fellow, but Crisp insisted that "he likes it."[5]

She soon "put all the pieces together," however. As Crisp explained to a reporter for the *Philadelphia Inquirer*: "I was in power, showing off my power to the staff, showing off sexuality in a nonthreatening way . . . and strutting my power. I know the feeling I had, the high I had. I was getting a big rush out of this." According to the report, Crisp apologized to the young man and has since used the story as an example of insensitive and illegal sexual harassment.[6]

In other reports of male harassment, the men have been pursued by women who apparently wanted to entice them into sexual affairs. Some men have filed complaints only to be told by a male consultant or a man in authority that they should consider themselves lucky to be so attractive to women. That points out the fact that men who claim sexual harassment may face some of the same difficulties that women have experienced for years. Even if a man suffers mental or physical abuse, he is not usually taken seriously or is considered "less than a man" for complaining.

However, some men have won lawsuits. One case made headlines in 1993 when a California man, Sabino Gutierrez, won over $1 million in a suit claiming harassment by his female supervisor, Maria Martinez. Gutierrez himself had had a history of sexually harassing females and had previously socialized with Martinez, with some reports indicating that they had once been lovers. Gutierrez also waited four years before he filed his suit against Martinez. But the case eventually was decided on the basis of who seemed to be more truthful, according to statements from jurors.

In spite of the unprecedented award, Gloria Allred, the attorney who represented Gutierrez, told reporters that instances of females harassing males are rare. "Sure it happens," she said, "but it's probably more likely as fiction."[7]

Legal Definitions of Sexual Harassment

Anecdotes illustrate in part what sexual harassment is and how people react to it. But there are countless variations in the types of behavior that are labeled sexual harassment, since people may experience and respond differently to sexual conduct, depending on their gender, age, and background. And in some cases the incidents may be same-sex harassment.

To begin with, sexual harassment is not the same thing as flirting or mutual sexual attraction—behavior based on choices that individuals make freely. And it is different from (although related to and sometimes intertwined with) other forms of harassment, such as the kind of bullying that is motivated by hatred for another's religious beliefs or racial heritage. Harassment of any type, sexual or otherwise, is action designed to persistently bother or torment someone. The verb *harass* actually stems from a French term meaning "to set a dog on."

Federal statutes and state codes now in force are based on a fairly basic definition of sexual harassment. Simply put, sexual harassment is a form of gender/sex discrimination that is prohibited by the Civil Rights Act of 1964; it is unwanted and unwelcome sexual behavior.

When that civil rights legislation was first proposed in the early 1960s, it banned job discrimination based on color, race, religion, or national origin. Opponents of the bill tried to block passage by adding what they considered was an absurd amendment, which banned sex discrimination. Many in Congress thought the amendment would lead to ridiculous lawsuits, but those who wanted the civil rights bill to become law voted in favor of it with the amendment intact.

A provision of the Civil Rights Act established the Equal Employment Opportunity Commission (EEOC) to administer the law. At first, the EEOC did not take the sex discrimination portion of the law seriously and for the most part ignored it. But throughout the 1970s groups working for women's rights pressured the EEOC to enforce the Civil Rights Act as it applied to discrimination based on gender. In addition, women's groups argued that sexual harassment, which was not defined or even mentioned in the Civil Rights Act, should be considered a form of sex discrimination.

It was not until 1980, however, that the EEOC explicitly defined sexual harassment as a form of illegal sex discrimination and issued guidelines on what constituted sexual harassment in the workplace. In 1984, the EEOC expanded the guidelines to include schools and issued a "Policy Statement on Sexual Harassment." A 1992 version of the policy statement declared, "Unwelcome sexual advances, requests for sexual favors, and other verbal or physical conduct of a sexual nature" constitute harassment, and such behavior is illegal "when submission to or rejection of this conduct explicitly or implicitly affects an individual's employment, unreasonably interferes with an individual's work performance or creates an intimidating, hostile or offensive work environment." The EEOC statement further pointed out that sexual harassment could occur in a variety of circumstances but emphasized that *unwelcome* conduct was a key to whether behavior could be found illegal.

In late 1993, the U.S. Supreme Court further defined on-the-job sexual harassment. The Court ruled in *Harris* v. *Forklift Systems Inc.* that, to have a legitimate claim, an alleged victim of harassment no longer had to prove that severe psychological trauma had resulted from the offensive behavior. Seven years earlier, the Supreme Court had determined that sexual harassment on the job was illegal if the conduct was severe or pervasive enough "to alter the conditions of the victim's employment," and lower circuit courts in several states interpreted that to mean anyone filing a sexual harassment suit had to show severe psychological injury. But with the 1993 decision, the High Court struck down such requirements. The case which led to that decision and other legal aspects of sexual harassment are covered in more detail in Chapter 4.

The definitions for sexual harassment in the workplace apply to school situations as well. Sexual harassment in schools is considered a form of sex discrimination. Title IX of the Education Amendments of 1972 states: "No person in the United States shall, on the basis of sex, be excluded from participation in, be denied the benefit of, or be subjected to discrimination under any program or activity receiving federal financial assistance."

In some situations, sex discrimination in schools may be gender stereotyping—of girls, primarily. That is, a teacher or administrator may victimize a girl by demeaning her, perhaps suggesting repeatedly that because of her gender she is not able to achieve. Female students may be consistently left out of class projects or discussions that center on such subjects as mathematics and science, or they may not be allowed to play sports that have long been thought of as "male only" domains. Such illegal discrimination results in self-doubt and lack of confidence among many girls and women.

When unwanted sexual behavior interferes with a person's education or ability to participate in school activities, it is sexual harassment and may be grounds for a lawsuit. For example, sexual harassment charges may be filed on behalf of a young girl whose education is disrupted because of the distress caused by a boy who snaps her bra, grabs her breasts, or calls her sexual names.

Lawsuits to obtain monetary awards for personal harm as well as compensation for job losses due to illegal sexual behavior have been widely publicized in recent years. As a result, many schools and workplaces have developed policies and programs to prevent sex discrimination and sexual harassment, since they could be liable if they fail to correct illegal discriminatory situations. People have generally become more aware of the problem, but education about what constitutes unwelcome and illegal sexual behavior is an ongoing process that is likely to continue for many years to come.

CHAPTER TWO

A "Dirty Little Secret"

Sex discrimination and sexual harassment are not new, as is clear from numerous stories told by women who have suppressed their experiences for decades. But as more and more women entered the workforce during the late 1960s, public attention began to focus on this type of aggressive behavior. With the passage of the Civil Rights Act of 1964, women were able to file lawsuits against those who discriminated against them because of their gender.

During the 1960s and early 1970s, women also aired their concerns about discriminatory practices and unwanted sexual attention with various women's groups, such as the National Organization for Women (NOW), the American Association of University Women, and 9to5—the National Association of Working Women. About the same time, studies and surveys of women workers (food service employees and United Nations workers, for example) showed that anywhere from 49 percent to over 55 percent had been the recipients of unwelcome sexual conduct while trying to do their jobs.

In November 1976, *Redbook* magazine published a major feature, "What Men Do to Women on the Job: A Shocking Look at Sexual Harassment," which included the results of a reader questionnaire. Of the 9,000 women who responded, 8,100 reported harassment of a sexual nature. The survey may not have been representative of all American women, since women with complaints were more likely to respond than those with no complaints. But the number of women filling out the questionnaire was significant nevertheless, since few women until that time had talked openly about or publicized what has been called the nation's "dirty little secret." Not only have sexual subjects been considered private matters; they have also been an embarrassment to discuss, particularly if women have been intimidated by threats of retaliation for reporting sexual misconduct on the job.

Not long after the publication of the *Redbook* survey, several books documenting sexual harassment called attention to the issue. *Sexual Shakedown: The Sexual Harassment of Women on the Job* (1978) by Lin Farley and *Sexual Harassment of Working Women: A Case of Sex Discrimination* (1979) by Catherine A. MacKinnon are examples of publications that helped create pressure to address a problem that appeared to be an ongoing, common occurrence in every type of workplace. Other studies, books, booklets, magazine articles, as well as conferences and lawsuits, followed, providing information and developing social and legal awareness of sexual harassment and its effects—not only at work but also in schools.

During the 1980s, when women's groups increasingly demanded enforcement of the Civil Rights Act of 1964, a number of court decisions awarded monetary damages to women who had been sexually harassed. Under the Civil Rights Act at that time, women could recover only lost wages. Nevertheless, in some sexual harassment cases, lawyers filed private lawsuits—common-law tort cases.

Tort law allows an individual who has been injured or whose property has been damaged to sue the person (the defendant) or persons causing the harm or damage. If the court finds the defendant to be at fault, that person must pay for the harm incurred. A case that attempts to show that a harasser has intentionally inflicted emotional distress "is one of the broadest common-law tort actions . . . and historically, the one most likely to secure money for harassed workers who have suffered mental anguish,"[1] according to attorneys William Petrocelli and Barbara Kate Repa.

In 1991, amendments to the Civil Rights Act (Title VII) provided victims of harassment with the means, under that law, to sue employers for damages to pay for personal harm and medical treatment as well as to compensate for loss of employment caused by harassment. But the Act placed limits on the amount of damages—from $50,000 to $300,000, depending on the number of employees in the company, ranging in increments from a minimum of fifteen to over five hundred. An employee working for a company with fewer than fifteen employees is not eligible to file a claim under the Civil Rights Act, although that employee may be able to take tort action.

A Visible Issue

Because of successful lawsuits, pressure from women's and other civil rights groups, and EEOC orders that companies must take "immediate and appropriate corrective action" in cases of sexual harassment, business leaders, school administrators, and government officials began to seriously look at and implement ways to prevent this type of discrimination. But the issue did not fully register on the public consciousness until the fall of 1991. At that time, the U.S. Senate Judiciary Committee convened to determine whether, as the Constitution requires, the Senate should confirm or deny the president's nomination of Clarence Thomas for U.S. Supreme Court justice. The nomination gained widespread attention because, after the resignation of the renowned justice Thurgood Marshall, Thomas would be the only black man on the High Court.

Thomas was practically assured the nomination, but rumors had been circulating that he had sexually harassed a black woman, Anita Hill, while both worked for the federal office of the Equal Employment Opportunity Commission (EEOC) during the 1980s. When nothing was done to investigate the rumors, public protest mounted, and the Judiciary Committee announced that it would hold televised hearings and would call Hill to testify.

Hill, who had long since left Washington, D.C., and had become a law professor at the University of Oklahoma, was grilled for hours by members of the committee—all of them white men. As the senators questioned Hill about the details of her story, the TV audience could hardly mistake the antagonistic manner of some senators, who clearly gave the impression that they thought Anita Hill was lying or was perhaps even psychologically unstable. For his part, Clarence Thomas vigorously denied all accusations, calling the hearings "a high-tech lynching" of a black man, and the Senate eventually voted to seat him on the Supreme Court.

Although some polls at the time showed that a majority of Americans believed Thomas rather than Hill, other polls later on indicated just the opposite. And thousands of women who saw or read about the hearings were outraged and began calling their congressional representatives and hotlines of women's organizations. As 9to5 explained:

> Throughout the country, sexual harassment became a matter of heated discussion. Countless women were moved to discuss their own harassment experiences publicly—often for the first time. . . . In trembling whispers or in voices boiling with anger, some recounted incidents that had occurred years or even decades earlier, while others asked what to do about the harasser sitting at the next desk.[2]

The Hill-Thomas or Thomas-Hill hearings, as they became known, prompted "a sea change . . . in the societal and corporate understanding of sexual harassment and the laws in place to stop it," Marcia Greenberger, co-president of the National Women's Law Center, noted several years later.[3]

Yet public debate over Anita Hill's testimony did not stop after the hearings. Charges and countercharges trying to discredit both Hill and Thomas appeared in all types of media, in part because of a long-standing link between sexism and racism in the United States. Some observers saw the outcome of the hearings as not only one more instance of his-word-against-hers-and-he-won, but also one more example of how women of color have been devalued and discredited for centuries.

Barbara Smith, who describes herself as "a black feminist," put it this way:

> The worst consequence of the Hill-Thomas hearings for me was in what they revealed about African Americans' level of consciousness regarding both sexual and racial politics. It has always taken courage for women of color to speak out about sexism within our own communities. In this instance it was done more publicly and dramatically than at any time in history. For that, Hill was attacked [by both whites and blacks].[4]

But there was another aspect. Because black men have historically been kept out of positions of power—whether in public or private life—many people of African-American ancestry defended Thomas. It appeared he was being victimized by the white power structure, and they worried that if he were not confirmed there would be little chance for a black person to serve on the High Court.

Black congresswoman Eleanor Holmes Norton, who represents Washington, D.C., noted: "Many blacks believed [Thomas] was all they could expect or get from a conservative president. . . . Even some blacks who distrusted Thomas and others who opposed him on his record saw a bird in the hand." In the end, however, "most African Americans did not support Thomas, and the nomination barely survived—by a vote of 52 to 48, the closest since 1888." According to Norton, "the majority of African Americans got past the race-sex confusion inherent in this conflict," and only 40 percent of the black community supported Thomas in what "seemed to be a take-it-or-leave-it proposition. Blacks did not squarely veto Thomas, but whites carried Thomas over."[5]

Not long after the hearings, a grassroots group called African American Women in Defense of Ourselves formed and placed an ad in *The New York Times* and other newspapers across the United States. In angry protest, the ad stated in part:

> Many have erroneously portrayed the allegations against Clarence Thomas as an issue of either gender or race. As women of African descent, we understand sexual harassment as both. We further understand that Clarence Thomas outrageously manipulated the legacy of lynching in order to shelter himself from Anita Hill's allegations. To deflect attention away from the reality of sexual abuse in African-American women's lives, he trivialized and misrepresented this painful part of African-American people's history. This country, which has a long legacy of racism and sexism, has never taken the sexual abuse of Black women seriously. . . . As Anita Hill's experience demonstrates, Black women who speak of these matters are not likely to be believed.[6]

Ever since that fall of 1991, Thomas defenders have fought back, and often they have appeared to be seeking revenge. In 1992, for example, David Brock, a reporter for the *Washington Times*, wrote a major feature for *The American Spectator* magazine in which he called Hill "a bit nutty and a bit slutty." The feature was part of a book released later in the year that attempted to discredit Hill.

However, the credibility of Brock's writings has been widely questioned. Critics have accused him of taking statements out of context and misrepresenting facts to bolster his point of view.

The Tailhook Scandal

Even before the 1991 congressional hearings, other sexual harassment charges—these involving the U.S. military—were made, although details of the case were not publicized until the summer of the following year. The incidents took place in September 1991 during a Las Vegas convention of naval aircraft-carrier fighter pilots, an annual event called Tailhook, named for the hook on the aircraft that snags and stops jets as they land on carriers.

More than five thousand Navy and Marine officers attended the weekend convention, which traditionally had been organized to bring retired and active-duty officers together for professional seminars, golf outings, and evening parties. Of the officers at the convention, only about 4 percent were women, among them Lieutenant Paula Coughlin, daughter of a career naval aviator. She had joined the Navy in 1984 and had been commissioned through the Navy's ROTC program at

Old Dominion University in Norfolk, Virginia. An aide to a rear admiral at the time of the convention, Coughlin had flown and tested a variety of aircraft and planned a long career as an aviator. She also held to a belief instilled by her family that Navy officers were honorable and heroic people. But all of that changed in Las Vegas.

Coughlin attended a formal dinner on Saturday, September 7, then later went to the third floor of the Hilton Hotel, where aviators had gathered for what Coughlin thought were cocktail parties in hospitality suites. She walked down a hall toward one of the suites with no clue as to what would happen next.

About two dozen pilots were lined along the hall, and one yelled "Admiral's aide!" apparently setting the stage for an attack. Coughlin was grabbed by the buttocks so forcefully that she was lifted off the floor. She angrily confronted the pilot who assaulted her, but others joined in the attack, grabbing her breasts and reaching under her skirt to pull at her underpants. Although she appealed for help, no one came to her aid and she was forced through another gauntlet. She was finally able to kick, claw, and bite her way free.

Coughlin was not the only officer abused. Dozens of female guests were assaulted, and some feared that they would be gang-raped. The next day Coughlin reported the attack to her immediate superior; then several other women over the next few weeks also went to Navy officials with reports of assaults. But months passed and no action was taken. Coughlin received no support from the Navy brass. Indeed, male officers were hostile toward her, and she was subjected to further sexual harassment by one official assigned to investigate the Tailhook incident.[7]

The Navy released a report of its investigation in April 1992, but only two suspects were identified. It was clear to some members of the U.S. Congress and to much of the public that the Navy was covering up the entire sordid mess. By June 1992, Coughlin, encouraged by her mother, who had spent twenty-seven years associated with the Navy as a career officer's wife, decided to speak to the press about the cover-up and the abuse of women that had gone unpunished.

What followed was a public scandal that prompted the resignation of the secretary of the Navy. The Office of the Inspector General of the U.S. Department of Defense reviewed the Navy's investigation of "Tailhook 91," as it was called, and in its first report, in 1992, stated that a failure of leadership had "created an atmosphere in which the assaults and other misconduct took place."[8]

A second report on Tailhook 91, released in April 1993, concluded that a total of eighty-three women had been assaulted. The report included graphic descriptions and photographs documenting the lewd, drunken behavior of male officers.[9]

By the end of 1993, one admiral had been reduced in rank and two others censured for failing to intervene to stop the Tailhook orgy. Thirty other admirals and about fifty junior officers were sent letters of caution about conduct unbecoming an officer, but there were no courts-martial and no one faced lawsuits for sexual harassment.

Meantime, though, Paula Coughlin was subjected to continued harassment, and in February 1994 she submitted her letter of resignation to the secretary of the Navy, explaining that the Tailhook assault and "the covert attacks on me that followed have stripped me of my ability to serve." While male officers were barely slapped on the wrist for their misconduct, Coughlin was forced to leave the military because of behavior of her male counterparts, sending what a *Los Angeles Times* editorial called "a chilling message to women."[10]

Charges Against a U.S. Senator

As the Tailhook story continued to emerge, another sexual harassment case made headlines. In 1992, *The Washington Post* published a report on sexual harassment charges that had been brought against Senator Bob Packwood of Oregon. In graphic detail, ten women, most of whom were former staff members, accused Packwood of unwelcome sexual advances, ranging from sudden, unwanted embraces to attempts to pull off a woman's clothes. Although Packwood at first denied the incidents, most of which occurred during the 1970s and early 1980s, he later issued a written apology for his behavior, which he attributed in part to a drinking problem.

Paige Wagers, one of the women who said she was sexually assaulted by Packwood on two occasions, called the public apology "a necessary first step." But in an article for a 1993 issue of the *National NOW Times*, Wagers noted that she is "still dealing with the repercussions" of the senator's behavior, as are some of the other women who said they were harmed by his actions.

"With limited resources, I am vulnerable to the slings and arrows of a powerful United States Senator," she wrote. "It is my hope that not only women across the country, but all decent people will unite to protest the seating of Packwood" (who was elected to a second term in the fall of 1992).

A group formed in Oregon to fight for Packwood's resignation. And the Women's Equal Rights Legal Defense and Education Fund made a formal request for a U.S. Senate Ethics Committee investigation. Such requests also were filed by other women's groups, and an inquiry began in 1993.

By early 1994, twelve other women had come forth with sexual harassment charges against Packwood. Yet many Oregon voters continued to support the senator, and some observers argued that his apology for past misbehavior should be enough, particularly since others in Congress have been accused of pressuring female employees for sexual favors.

CHAPTER THREE
Power Plays

For centuries, women and girls have received the "chilling message" that they are not welcome in positions of power in male-dominated institutions— whether connected with the military, business, education, government, religion, or the family. Although women ruled some ancient societies and were honored as priestesses or as goddesses, they have generally been viewed as underlings throughout most of the world's history. In fact, until recent times, most nations denied women and girls any rights and considered them no more than chattel—property that by law and custom belonged to their husbands or fathers.

Religious beliefs have played a major role in suppressing women, as male religious scholars developed theories contending that women were born to be subservient caregivers. In other male-dominated disciplines, from biology to sociology, many experts have insisted that it is a woman's "nature" to "surrender" to a man, and that she should be guided by the "superior" intellect of men and should be ruled by a patriarch—the senior male member of a family who protects and provides for women and children. Such views are still circulated widely today and have helped support the age-old myth that only men should be in charge.

Even in nations like the United States, Canada, and Great Britain, where women have gained legal rights over the past century or so, they were once denied educations, jobs, property and voting rights, and countless other privileges that men have enjoyed over the ages. Men as a rule have maintained power over most aspects of society and thus women's lives, a fact that has been increasingly recognized in sexual harassment cases that have been brought before the courts.

An Abuse of Power

Power over women has led to a great many discriminatory practices designed to keep women in passive roles. The male hold on power also has led to sexual harassment, which by most definitions is an abuse of power based on gender. That is, in order to stay in control, some men use sexual harassment as a way to insult, demean, or intimidate women who do not have the money, status, or authority to retaliate.

Some men harass to "keep women in their place," as they say. That is, they adhere to a philosophy of male dominance that has existed for centuries. They believe, as John Adams said in the 1770s, that "nature has made them [women] fittest for domestic cares," and that women are of value only in subordinate roles. Of course, today there certainly are many men of all ages who do *not* hold such views and who staunchly repudiate them.

When a man sexually harasses a woman, he may do so because he resents a woman who is independent. He may want to punish her for not accepting the homemaker-caregiver role. Or he may believe that since he is a man, he has a "right" to certain kinds of employment, but a woman does not. Or he may believe that a woman has a right to work at any type of job outside the home but that she is subject to his rule when in "his" domain. As a result, a man may assault a woman physically and verbally.

Consider Sandra Huffman, a woman in her twenties who worked in 1991–1992 on the loading dock at a Pepsi Cola plant in Burnsville, Minnesota, a suburb of Minneapolis. Because her male coworkers did not want her on the job, they repeatedly taunted her with sexual ridicule, including a display of lewd photographs of women that her coworkers had labeled with Huffman's name. Huffman's car was also vandalized. But the worst insult came one day when two male coworkers physically assaulted her by reaching inside her coveralls to fondle her. She quit her job the next day and soon filed a lawsuit against the male coworkers and the company that allowed the unwelcome sexual behavior to continue. In February 1994, a jury found that Huffman was forced to leave her job because of sexual harassment and awarded her $530,000 in actual and punitive damages.[1]

A less obvious form of power abuse occurs when men—and women too—fail to recognize that a person is much more than her or his biological makeup. Whatever their gender, vast numbers of Americans as well as people in other countries have been taught to believe that females are less capable than males. Consequently the potential of women and girls is often ignored or overlooked and females are excluded from positions of power.

One common example of this type of exclusion was prevalent for years in all-male service organizations such as the Rotary Club, Kiwanis, and Lions. Because they were kept out of these groups, women were unable to gain access to the "old-boy networks" by which men promoted each other in the job market and in business dealings—until federal civil rights laws were enforced in the 1980s to require the groups to admit women.

In spite of legal bans on discrimination, women in the workplace are not usually welcome at social or recreational events, such as golf outings, that have been traditionally all-male. Such barriers have long handicapped women who want to advance in the workplace or make contacts that would help them improve their financial well-being. Without high economic status, women are frequently seen as dependent on men for part or all of their income—even though the women may be supporting themselves and their families.

In politics similar stereotypes prevail. Based only on myths about women's lack of leadership abilities, some voters—both male and female—may conclude that women are unable to make tough decisions and govern effectively. Voters with such a gender bias would likely cast their ballots for men. Nevertheless, women in the United States have been able to win elections to political office at the local, state, and federal levels on a fairly regular basis in recent years. In 1993, for example, women held 22 percent of the 324 elective state offices, according to the Center for the American Woman and Politics at Rutgers University.[2]

But the percentage of women in top governmental positions is small. Women compose more than half of the population, but in the 103rd Congress made up only 7 percent of the Senate and only 11 percent of the House—55 out of a total of 535 seats. Clearly, men have maintained their hold on governmental power.

Sexist Attitudes and Gender Roles

The male grip on the power structure in government and other areas of society is supported by sexism—viewing people in specific roles based on their gender. Sexism is also a form of stereotyping: making a judgment about a person's abilities and behavior based on the particular group of which she or he is a part (whether that group is categorized by gender, color, religion, or nationality).

One stereotype about women assumes that they are born "weak" and in need of male protection. Yet anthropologists studying ancient cultures have found that women developed strong, muscular bodies when they had to search for food, carry heavy loads of water and timber for building materials, and do other jobs requiring physical exertion. In more recent history, when women were needed outside the home—during World Wars I and II, for example—they were encouraged to do so-called men's work and take jobs in factories and on farms.

In spite of their abilities and accomplishments, women as a group worldwide are considered second-class citizens. This view has remained fairly constant because of sexism and stereotyping. Children, for example, are taught early in life to assume roles based on their gender. Toys children play with, the language they learn, and the images they see of their gender in the mass media reinforce what is considered appropriate feminine or masculine behaviors and attitudes.

Certainly some genetic differences between boys and girls may affect the way each gender behaves. But gender-based roles are primarily determined by a culture—the way of life of a group of people—and those roles are so entrenched that it is difficult to counteract them. Consider sports. Generally, boys are encouraged to get involved in all types of sports, to join teams or to participate in individual sports or in rough-and-tumble activities, while the majority of girls are encouraged to shy away from what has been deemed "male behavior." Yet girls and women who have participated in sports have for the most part reaped the same types of benefits that men have—they feel more in control and have higher self-esteem and healthier mental attitudes than those who do not compete on the playing field.

Ellen Lewis, a TV producer and young mother in New York City, described in an article for *The New York Times Magazine* some of the barriers that parents must overcome to help their children at an early age get beyond rigid behavior patterns assigned according to gender. While attending a block party, her three-year-old daughter won a game, and the woman in charge of the event offered a doll as a prize. But Lewis put the doll back in the prize box and let her daughter make her own choice, which was a "plastic racket with a ball attached to it by elastic." Although Lewis acknowledged that she sometimes goes along with the gender stereotyping (such as complying with a friend's request to get "anything with four wheels" for a little boy's birthday gift), she makes special efforts to "avoid generalizing about boys' and girls' behavior" and encourages her daughters to play with "trucks and tools, along with doll houses and toy stoves."[3]

Lewis wrote that she was the exception among her peers in terms of her parenting concepts. In fact, her friends were convinced that behavior differences in their children were genetically based. Although such views may be in the majority across the United States, other young parents like Lewis are trying to steer their children away from rigid gender-based roles. In Port Townsend, Washington, for example, the director of a computer-education program in a magnet school and father of a three-year-old son said:

> Our household is set up differently from the majority of homes in North America. I stay home most of the time to write, while my wife's business takes her out into the public arena virtually every day. Because of this arrangement, I have accepted the main responsibility for completing the home chores: vacuuming, washing the clothes, grocery shopping, cooking, and paying the bills. My son's independent play time tends to revolve around these duties, which I find any good homemaker has to accomplish. And since I want him to start to take responsibility for the maintenance of his own life, he often helps me to get these things done. He follows me or his mother around with a toy vacuum as we use the real thing on the carpet. He's

become pretty adept at baking bread too. Of course, he has his own apron.

In our house, the boy sees that working on the computer, cleaning the toilet, washing the dirty clothes, mowing the lawn, and watching a baseball game on TV are acceptable human behavior. Nevertheless, it is interesting that many times we tend to relate to each other as my father used to relate to me. We kiss and hug and cuddle, but I'm more than likely to break that off with some sort of rough-housing, teasing behavior. Our role-playing games often revolve around the modeling of more assertive types of behavior. And while I tended to act in these same ways with my daughter, who's a teenager, her behavior patterns became more "typical female." Still, I'm convinced that the tasks that we complete in this life (other than the obvious sexual ones) have nothing to do with our chromosomes.[4]

Male and Female Perceptions

As youngsters mature, peer pressure, social customs, educational systems, and religious and political institutions contribute to a gender-specific kind of socialization. Differences in the way girls and boys are socialized then can lead to a general acceptance of certain types of behavior for boys and other types for girls, which helps perpetuate gender discrimination and sexual harassment.

For example, it has been commonly believed that women and girls "provoke" or invite sexual remarks and assaults. If girls are taught that they must dress and behave "properly" to assure that they will be treated with respect, they may assume that they are responsible if they are sexually harassed. Even now, such myths prevail. But the fact is that sexual harassment occurs no matter how girls and women dress. For example, women in uniforms and conservative dresses or suits have been harassed.

In some cases, men and boys who have been accused of sexual misconduct have not been aware that their behavior was unwelcome. Throughout their early childhood and high school years, behavior such as sexually explicit name-calling, groping and pinching girls, or taking part in "flip-up day"—a playground ritual in which boys pull up girls' skirts—may never have been criticized. In fact, many adults have accepted such conduct, rationalizing that if they make too much of the situation matters will get worse.

Phyllis Lerner, who serves as a consultant to the Gender Equity Office for the California State Department of Education, travels the United States to talk to school groups about gender equity and was "aghast" to find that many parents and educators shrugged off flip-up day as a harmless prank. One parent said such actions were OK because the girls simply wear shorts under their skirts. But Lerner noted in an interview with a *Los Angeles Times* reporter in 1993 that the "prank" is a prime example of gender inequity. After all, girls don't traditionally participate in a day when they pull down boys' pants. Flip-up day reinforces the concept that it is all right to show disrespect for girls and to harass them with inappropriate sexual behavior. In Lerner's view, "There's a lot of stuff going on in our schools that I term sexual hasslement that matures into sexual harassment."[5]

"Hasslement" on the Street

Another type of "sexual hasslement" occurs on the street. For sixteen-year-old Beth from southern California, one experience of street harassment took place while she was visiting Chicago. It was a hot, muggy July day, and Beth, like many tourists, was wearing shorts as she strolled along the sidewalk window-shopping with her grandmother. It was lunchtime, and as she walked past a group of construction workers sitting on a low wall outside a parking garage, a slow, subdued "hel-looooo" began, changing to a "wooooo" that rose in a crescendo. The bellow from the "sitting bulls" was echoed on the other side of the street by another group of construction workers.

"It was like walking the gauntlet," Beth said. "My face turned red. I felt like crawling. I clutched the jacket I'd brought with me, balling it up in front of me, and almost ran a full block to get away from those guys."[6]

Beth was the target of male behavior that has been going on for generations, with young men usually imitating the actions of their peers, fathers or uncles or even grandfathers. In urban and rural areas across the United States, millions of girls and women are subjected to street harassment, which is probably one of the most difficult kinds of harassment to prevent or stop.

This behavior persists partly because most women have been taught to believe that being whistled, wowed, or wooed at by men is complimentary. And few people—men or women—actually think of these actions as harmful. But as Beth's grandmother pointed out: "My granddaughter and I were minding our own business, walking in a public place, and it made me angry to see and hear those creeps treat a pretty, young girl like she was a nonperson. She was uncomfortable and I was uncomfortable."[7]

Discomfort is just one reaction that street harassment victims experience, and that discomfort is usually more oppressive when a woman is subjected to lewd, sexual comments about her body or is propositioned in gutter terms. Even more distressing for women is being pinched, touched, or stroked while passing a male molester on the street.

While it is commonly believed that street harassment is not a serious problem, women who have experienced it often feel intimidated, according to a 1992 survey by *Glamour* magazine. Staff writer Elizabeth Kuster found: "A woman who is confronted with a barrage of male commentary whenever she ventures outside is constantly on edge in public. Even such a small act as walking to the corner to mail a letter can create anxiety. There is a cumulative effect of such constant humiliation."[8]

If a woman has been subjected to a steady buildup of embarrassing and sometimes frightening encounters in public places, she frequently takes protective measures, such as avoiding construction sites where there are likely to be groups of men, or wearing cover-up clothing (such as a coat or long jacket), or hiding behind sunglasses, or walking in a brisk, businesslike manner. In short, a woman loses some of her freedom and sometimes her self-esteem because of unwanted street harassment.

Media Support for Discrimination

Perhaps one of the most insidious factors contributing to the practice of gender stereotyping and sexual harassment is the media portrayal of women and girls. Seldom are females shown as people of intellect or as strong, responsible persons. Instead, males are shown in those roles, and women are usually shown as subordinates, sometimes silly, usually eager to please as they clean, cook, care for kids and husbands—in spite of the fact that nearly 75 percent of women aged twenty to forty-four work outside the home. In addition, many TV shows and movies depict women as victims of assault, rape, murder, and harassment, often giving the impression that all women are prey and in danger of physical attacks.

The advertising, TV, and film media also focus overwhelmingly on sexually attractive women, presenting images that support the current notion of what females should look like: sex objects rather than multifaceted persons who can achieve in a variety of fields. Girls and women are then expected to pattern themselves after an ideal image of beauty that has been established primarily by men and is subject to male approval.

"That focus on beauty keeps women away from a sense that if they work hard to achieve a goal, they'll be rewarded," according to Naomi Wolf, author of *The Beauty Myth* and other works on women's issues. In a

March 1994 interview for *Women's Sports & Fitness,* Wolf pointed out how women in just one field, sports, usually must fit the model of "a conventionally beautiful person" in order to be selected for advertising and promotional campaigns. Appearance seems to be the most important factor for the chosen athletes, which, in Wolf's words, sends "the message that [advertisers] don't care whether women achieve or fail on their own terms. We as consumers have a responsibility to insist that the people who get rewarded and highlighted by corporations are indeed the best athletes."9

As media images continue to dictate what is beautiful and sexually appealing, many girls and women face a double bind in terms of their appearance. If they choose to wear sexually attractive clothes, they may be subjected to harassment because the common myth is that "they asked for it"—they dressed in ways to provoke sexual comments, assaults, or even rape. If, on the other hand, women and girls wear conservative clothing, they may be taunted by males—fellow workers or students—because they are not more provocative.

"Woman-as-sex-object" is the unmistakable theme in many music videos and movies. In these media, women and girls are commodities that men use for their own purposes or sell to the highest bidder or "give away" as a token of appreciation to other men. Such exploitation of women and girls has been the subject of various types of literature for centuries, but a number of recent films released in the 1990s have been based on the women-as-property concept. *Indecent Proposal,* for example, starred Robert Redford as a billionaire who offered to pay a young couple (Woody Harrelson and Demi Moore) $1 million as payment for one night with the wife. The story line was supposedly based on an ethical dilemma: Should a couple who need money accept the offer, and if they do what would be the consequences to their relationship? Little is said about the ethics of one person selling or buying another.

Some movie critics, professors of literature and film, and other commentators see *Indecent Proposal* and movies with similar story lines (*Pretty Woman, Honeymoon in Vegas,* and *Mad Dog and Glory* are examples) as a reflection of the uncertainty people feel about the changing social structure. It is "part of a backlash" against women who are independent or are trying to be, according to Gloria Kaufman, director of women's studies at Indiana University South Bend. "Women are really beginning to move into the board-room, and there is a resentment among men."[10]

In Kaufman's view, that resentment has not manifested itself as a conspiracy by male filmmakers to blast or destroy women, but instead reflects widely held opinions about the low status of women. Perhaps, as the old saying goes, most people can be "bought for a price," but the fact remains that women (and sometimes men) who can be sold or traded are seldom valued as persons but rather as items to be auctioned in the marketplace.

CHAPTER FOUR

Harassment at Work

"Complaints are mounting, confusion is rampant, and almost everybody's a little nervous," declared a sub-head for a 1993 *Fortune* magazine article on sexual harassment in the workplace. According to the report, "90 percent of Fortune 500 companies have dealt with sexual harassment complaints. More than a third have been sued at least once, and about a quarter have been sued over and over again."[1]

In early 1993 the *Dallas Morning News* reported that a statewide poll showed "almost a fourth of all Texans and a third of Texas women . . . [had] been sexually intimidated at work. . . . Of the women who reported being intimidated or pursued at work, more than half said the incidents contributed to [their] leaving their jobs or wanting to."[2] A *Time* magazine report noted that since 1991, "federal sexual-harassment complaints have nearly doubled, from 6,892 in 1991 to 12,537 in 1993."[3]

Increasingly, women in male-dominated trade jobs such as construction; in professional fields like the performing arts, the sciences, law, and medicine; in governmental offices; and in religious institutions have reported their experiences with sexual harassment. The Tailhook scandal called attention to sexual harassment in the military, where there have been steady reports from women who have been the targets of unwelcome sexual behavior by male senior officers. Similar reports have come from female lawyers and law enforcement agents.

Do the statistics and increasing number of sexual harassment reports mean that discrimination based on gender is more common in the workplace today than in years past? No one is certain about the answer. In the first place, the workforce has been changing rapidly. More and more women have started working alongside men on the job, which is one factor contributing to the rise of sexual harassment cases. Another is the changing attitudes of girls and women. In the past, women generally did not discuss sexual matters even with their best friends; now many women are beginning to speak out about sexual abuses and discrimination they face in the workplace. As many have asked rhetorically: "If male employees do not have to put up with sexual comments and assault and verbal put-downs, then why should female employees have to endure such behavior on the job?"

Defining Harassment in the Workplace

Just about every place where men and women are on the job together is a potential site for sexual intimidation. Although many companies and institutions have taken steps to prevent gender-based discrimination, hundreds of reported incidents in recent years have called attention to inappropriate sexual behavior in the workplace. Cases vary considerably, but in general there are two types of behavior that the EEOC and the courts have determined are illegal.

The most obvious abuse of power is a situation in which a person in authority (usually a male in a supervisory position or the boss) intimidates a female employee, demanding sexual favors in return for letting her keep her job or gain a promotion. This is often called quid pro quo, a Latin term that basically means giving something in exchange for something else—in this case sex for a job, as it is known in the harassment vernacular. In one such case (*Rodolakis* v. *Rudomin*) decided by a Massachusetts court in January 1994, a jury awarded $1 million to an employee who had filed a lawsuit claiming that in order to keep her job, she had been forced by her supervisor to have sex with him in his office once or twice a week over a twenty-month period.

Another type of harassment is termed "hostile (or poisoned) environment." The Northwest Women's Law Center listed examples of what constitutes "hostile environment" harassment:

- Making sexually suggestive remarks, gestures, or jokes
- Making offensive, negative remarks about the victim's gender or physical appearance
- Using derogatory sexual terms for women such as honey, baby, chick, bitch, etc.
- Deliberate touching, pinching, brushing, or patting
- Displaying offensive sexual illustrations

- Pressuring for dates or sex
- Describing or asking about personal sexual experiences
- Hazing, pranks, or other intimidating behavior directed toward the victim because of the victim's gender[4]

These types of harassment are common in workplaces that traditionally have been all-male. Male workers may harass women to force them off the job, or they may make it difficult for a woman to do her job. In a hostile environment, a female worker may be harmed by repeated offensive behavior that creates psychological stress, fear of physical danger, or another damaging reaction that interferes with her job performance.

In one case, Sandra Hernandez, an agent with the Bureau of Alcohol, Tobacco and Firearms, testified in a Civil Service Commission hearing in Chicago during July 1993 that she was harassed by her training officer, John Gamboa. According to Hernandez's testimony, Gamboa was her training agent in 1990 and led her "to believe he was very powerful," so she kept silent about his sexual misconduct—touching, grabbing, kissing, hugging—because she feared she would be fired. She also testified that she told her supervisor his behavior was unwelcome, and she refused his request to buy sexy clothing or to wear a miniskirt to work. Gamboa was dismissed in 1992, but he insisted that Hernandez's charges were false.[5]

Reports of sexually motivated discrimination in law enforcement have come from large and small police departments across the nation. "Hostility toward women is entrenched" and "has until recently gone virtually unchecked" in the Los Angeles Police Department, according to a March 1994 report in the *Los Angeles Times*. The newspaper cited court records, internal police documents, and interviews with police officers, supervisors, and department critics that revealed that women in the department had reported unwelcome sexual behavior ranging "from a sexually explicit computer program left in the terminals of female officers, to supervisors who press subordinates for dates, to three pending lawsuits involving claims that officers raped colleagues."[6]

Some policewomen said they had put up with unwelcome sexual behavior for years because they feared retaliation, such as further attacks by a harasser or lack of backup help when needed on the job, a life-threatening situation. They were convinced that antagonism and bias toward women would continue to be ignored as it had been for years, although Los Angeles police chief Willie L. Williams began to address the problem and promised aggressive action to prevent discrimination against women in the department.

Harassment of women is also widespread in the medical profession, a fact that came to public attention in 1991 when Frances Conley, the first female neurosurgeon at Stanford Medical School, wrote a newspaper editorial describing her experiences and those of female medical students. Without naming anyone, Conley explained in detail how women had to endure unwelcome sexual behavior (from suggestive comments to fondling and other demeaning acts) from male doctors or students, "going along to get along," as many women have been forced to do or lose the opportunity to advance in a chosen career.

Most of the responses to Conley's editorial were supportive; they came from both male and female staff and students, as well as from hundreds of people in various types of employment across the United States. Conley had planned to resign from the university, but she withdrew her resignation when Stanford administrators began to seriously investigate reports of sexual harassment. Yet since Conley's complaints were aired, other women at Stanford Medical School have charged male doctors with sexual harassment, and one filed a lawsuit in May 1994.[7]

Although some medical facilities have become more responsive to complaints about sexual harassment of women doctors, nearly 75 percent of female medical students surveyed for a 1993 report published in *The New England Journal of Medicine* said they were harassed. Eleven of the forty-nine men in the survey were subjected to harassment, usually by male physicians.[8]

Another survey published in the *Journal* showed that female doctors are also sexually harassed by their male patients. Of the 422 female physicians responding in the survey, 77 percent of the women, who were between the ages of twenty-four and sixty-four, were harassed. Although some reported being amused or indifferent to the behavior, 35 percent were angry about the incidents and 26 percent were frightened.[9]

Court Decisions

To determine whether there is a hostile work environment, the EEOC and the courts have based their decisions on what is known as the "reasonable woman" (or "reasonable person") standard. This standard was first established by the U.S. Court of Appeals for the Ninth

Circuit in a 1991 case, *Ellison* v. *Brady*. Kelly Ellison, an Internal Revenue Service agent, sued a colleague who pressured her for dates in spite of her consistent refusals; the colleague also sent her "love letters," which Ellison considered weird and frightening. Although a district court dismissed the case as "trivial," the Ninth Circuit Court declared that Ellison had suffered "severe and pervasive" harassment, noting:

> Conduct that many men consider unobjectionable may offend many women. Because women are disproportionately victims of rape and sexual assault, women have a stronger incentive to be concerned with sexual behavior. Women who are victims of mild forms of sexual harassment may understandably worry whether a harasser's conduct is merely a prelude to a violent sexual assault. Men, who are rarely victims of sexual assault, may view sexual conduct in a vacuum without a full appreciation of the social setting or the underlying threat of violence that a woman may perceive.[10]

The differences in the way men and women perceive offensive behavior were outlined in *The Washington Post* by columnist Bob Levey. In early 1994, Levey wrote several columns about the crude behavior of many car salesmen and their attitudes toward saleswomen. According to Levey, "One saleswoman said that in her sales salon, the F-word is in the air constantly. Another said she was told to 'go home and do the dishes' if she didn't like it." A salesman on the other hand told Levey that "the F-word epidemic in car dealerships is just the way guys and the auto business are."

One saleswoman who had worked for a car dealership for four years reported that it was common practice for salesmen to hire strippers to "come in during business hours, completely disrobe and perform suggestive acts with them. These episodes took place anywhere: the service lane, the wash bays, the lunchroom!" When the saleswoman objected, she was told she had no sense of humor.[11]

Although this saleswoman might have had a legitimate claim that lewd behavior made the workplace a hostile environment, she would have been required by law to prove that the offensive behavior interfered with her job and that she had reported the sexual misconduct to her employer, who then did nothing effective to stop it. That was how Carol Zabkowicz, a warehouse worker, won her sexual harassment suit. As described in *The 9to5 Guide to Combating Sexual Harassment*, Carol

> was tormented by a group of male coworkers who enjoyed upsetting her by calling out her name and then exposing their genitals or buttocks when she looked up. Carol complained to management, to no avail. . . . Even when she brought witnesses with her and submitted evidence in the form of obscene cartoons that had been left at her workstation, management did nothing. When the case went to court, the company was found guilty of "malicious, blatant discrimination."[12]

The U.S. Supreme Court further defined a hostile or abusive workplace environment when it ruled in November 1993 in behalf of Teresa Harris, a former manager for Forklift Systems in Nashville, Tennessee. Harris quit her job because the owner of the company, Charles Hardy, constantly subjected her to boorish comments—for example, suggesting on several occasions in public that she traded sex for sales contracts. Hardy also tried to negotiate sexual favors from Harris by promising her a pay raise, and tried to convince Harris to take coins from the front pockets of his pants.

Harris filed a lawsuit (*Harris v. Forklift Systems Inc.*) in 1987 charging that she was compelled to leave her job because of sexual harassment. A district court dismissed the charges, ruling that Harris had not suffered any severe psychological damage and her job performance had not suffered, and concluding that she could not sue even though Hardy's behavior would be considered vulgar by most reasonable people. But after six years of appeals, the High Court overturned the lower court ruling and required that the case be judged by new standards: Even if an employee is not psychologically harmed and her job performance does not suffer, she may be in a hostile working environment if she is prevented from job advancement or discouraged from staying on the job. Even with the new standard, however, Justice Sandra Day O'Connor cautioned that there is no "precise test" for a sexually discriminating work environment and that "all the circumstances" must be considered.

Critics of the U.S. Supreme Court decision in *Harris* say the ruling now makes companies and institutions liable for behavior considered annoying, crude, disrespectful, humiliating, and insensitive. But recent cases that have been reported or brought before the courts show that if a business takes prompt action to stop harassment and eliminate a hostile environment, it is not liable for the sexual misconduct of employees. That was the decision in a lawsuit filed by Denise Nash, a clerk working for Electrospace System Inc. (ESI) of Texas (*Nash v. Electrospace System Inc.*).

Nash claimed in 1993 that three years earlier her supervisor, John Sharp, had begun to ask her questions about her personal life. According to a description of the case in a Bureau of National Affairs (BNA) publication, "Nash was offended by the sexual nature of the questions, although Sharp did not demand sexual favors as a condition of employment." (Although he was a supervisor, Sharp did not have the authority to hire or fire.) Nash also claimed in her suit that she had "received several sexually suggestive, anonymous telephone calls, which she believed Sharp made." But Nash did not make a complaint about the alleged harassment until February 1991.

ESI's human resources director investigated the charges immediately and "told Sharp not to converse with Nash, and finally transferred Nash to another department." Although Nash said the transfer was in retaliation for filing a complaint with the EEOC, the court declared the company had investigated promptly and had transferred Nash to an equivalent job within one week, which "represented a prudent response" and was a "model of prompt, sensitive employer handling" of a traumatic situation. The company was not held liable for the charges of sexual harassment.[13]

Effects of Sexual Discrimination

Although some court cases are widely publicized, most women who are sexually harassed do not file lawsuits or even report the incidents—only 1 to 7 percent file complaints.[14] Why? Because when women make complaints or file lawsuits they frequently must defend themselves against countercharges that their claims are fraudulent. This is true for nearly all "whistle-blowers"—those who report wrongdoing in a workplace.

Employees who charge harassment also fear retaliation from supervisors and alienation from other workers, according to testimony during a U.S. congressional hearing held in March 1994. Congressman William L. Clay of Missouri, chairman of the House Post Office and Civil Service Subcommittee on Oversight and Investigations, called the hearing because, he said, "Sexual harassment is a pervasive, apparently intractable problem in the federal workplace."

Gail Wyche, a special agent with the Drug Enforcement Administration in Albuquerque, New Mexico, testified that her first experience with sexual harassment occurred when she went to a supervisor about a discrimination problem on the job. When the problem was not solved, Wyche went through the appropriate channels to a supervisor on a higher level. That person promised to take care of the problem on the condition that he and Wyche "would go barhopping [and] hot tubbing together on a weekly basis." Wyche then filed a sexual harassment claim, but investigators "displayed an insensitive and apathetic attitude towards me and treated me as if I was the perpetrator of the harassment rather than the victim," she testified.[15]

Because many women who make sexual harassment complaints are treated as if they were to blame or are discredited as "unstable" or as "troublemakers," their frustration and anger may build. That in turn can lead to stress-related illnesses: chronic headaches and fatigue, intestinal problems, loss of appetite and sleep, and frequent infections. Such problems can cause them to miss work, perform poorly, and perhaps even be fired.

Absenteeism, employee turnover, and low productivity due to harassment "cost the typical Fortune 500 company $6.7 million," according to a business analysis of a *Working Woman* survey on harassment that brought 9,680 reader responses.[16] In addition, sexual discrimination and harassment lawsuits can be expensive for companies and businesses. No matter what the outcome of a suit, time and money must be spent on defense.

However, there have been some positive results as sexual discrimination and harassment cases have been more widely publicized. Because of their experiences with sexual harassment, some women have set up consultant or litigation firms to aid female workers who are whistle-blowers. And many firms have realized that they can no longer ignore discriminatory practices against women and have begun to establish preventive policies.

Workplace Policies

Companies know that policies and programs to prevent sexual harassment and discrimination will help reduce costs. But there are other reasons for such efforts. One is changing demographics. Labor experts predict a shrinking workforce in the United States, and most of the new workers today are women. If women leave their jobs because of harassment, companies could suffer labor shortages. In addition, by the year 2000, the workforce is expected to be 50 percent female, and an increase in numbers often translates into power. Feeling empowered, women may be inspired even more to assert their rights.

Many employers are trying to educate their workers, requiring employees to attend seminars or workshops to learn what constitutes a hostile environment and sexual harassment. Lawyers and consultants who conduct such seminars say that while some employees welcome the guidelines as a way to avoid problems, sometimes it is difficult to put across the message about what is or is not acceptable behavior in the workplace. Some would suggest eliminating all sexual interaction—flirting or sexual bantering, for example.

Some research suggests a correlation between sexual interaction and sexual harassment, and it provides some support for the idea that prohibiting sexual interaction is a sound strategy for stopping illegal sexual harassment. But Brian Baigrie, a philosopher working in the field of social sciences at the University of Toronto, Canada, is not persuaded by that argument.

> What it presumes is that sexual interaction is somehow to blame. . . . A more plausible explanation, in my view, is that many in the workplace are unable to distinguish positive sexual interaction from unwanted sexual attention. We need to work hard at educating ourselves about this distinction . . . to ensure that we do not give in to the impulse to regulate all sexual behavior, even that which is admittedly positive and constructive.[17]

One barrier to the educational process is the depiction, on TV and in other media, of sexual harassment on the job as routine and acceptable. Another is a great resistance to change, especially in male-dominated workplaces. In fact, there have been numerous reports of male employees who not only continue to harass but also retaliate against female workers—by sending them lewd messages, for example, or showing pornographic movies in the workplace, or simply being uncooperative and openly hostile to women on the job.

Nevertheless, stronger enforcement of Title VII of the federal Civil Rights Act has pushed companies to try to eliminate sexual harassment in the workplace. A few states—California, Maine, Minnesota, and Washington among them—have passed laws that require employers to take action on sexual harassment complaints. Other states are considering such legislation.

In New York, Governor Mario M. Cuomo proposed legislation based on a task force report released in January 1994. Cuomo set up the thirty-four-member task force after the confirmation hearings for U.S. Supreme Court justice Clarence Thomas, and the group spent eighteen months researching sexual harassment in workplaces and schools. Its report included fifty-seven recommendations, including mandatory workplace policies prohibiting harassment and education and training about sexual harassment. "Unequivocally . . . the single most important solution to sexual harassment is prevention," the task force concluded. "After-the-fact remedies are, at best, patchwork solutions that are available only after the harm has occurred."[18]

CHAPTER FIVE

Harassment at School

While employers attempt to prevent sexual harassment in the workplace, many parents and school personnel are trying to stop unwelcome sexual behavior in schools, on school grounds, and at school-sponsored events, such as athletic competitions, field trips, concerts, and plays. Sexual harassment in schools has become an explosive issue, not only because of increased public awareness of the problem but also because of a U.S. Supreme Court decision in 1992.

That year the High Court heard a case (*Franklin* v. *Gwinnett County Public Schools*) in which a Georgia teenager charged that a teacher had consistently harassed her during a time when she helped him grade papers. According to the suit, the teacher wanted to know about the teenager's sex life, discussed his own, and eventually persuaded her to have sex with him. The justices ruled in favor of the teenager and unanimously declared that students can be awarded monetary damages for sex discrimination and sexual harassment under Title IX of the Education Amendments of 1972—the federal law prohibiting sex discrimination, including sexual harassment, in any educational institution or program that receives federal funds.

Prior to the 1992 decision, students could file lawsuits under Title IX, but if successful the only monetary awards they could receive would be for lost wages, as stipulated by the law—obviously of little value to students who are not employed by the school. Since the court decision in the Georgia case, sexual harassment complaints to the Department of Education's Office of Civil Rights, which oversees the enforcement of Title IX, reportedly increased almost fourfold, from 40 in 1991 to 156 at the end of 1993.[1]

Peer Harassment

Sexual harassment of students by teachers or others in authority is just one issue in the schools today. More commonly, students have complained about unwelcome and unwanted sexual conduct on the part of another student (or several students). Incidents have been reported from diverse areas of the nation:

• In 1988, when Tawyna Brawdy was in eighth grade in Petaluma, California, she had to face a group of fifteen to thirty boys at school who "mooed" and taunted her about the size of her breasts. She tried to ignore the behavior, but, she reported, "It happened before school, in classes, during lunch, after school. . . . At times I got phone calls." According to a news report, "Tawyna and her mother appealed to teachers, the principal, the superintendent to stop the harassment, but no action was taken." One teacher sympathized but told Tawyna she "would have to live with" the boys' taunting. However, Tawyna and her mother filed a civil rights complaint in 1989, charging the school with creating a hostile environment. The Brawdys were awarded $20,000 in an out-of-court settlement.[2]

• In Duluth, Minnesota, Katy Lyle learned in 1988 when she was in high school that sexually explicit graffiti about her had been scrawled in one of the boys' bathrooms. She had no idea who was responsible for the act or why it was done. The graffiti remained for eighteen months, in spite of numerous complaints that Katy made to school authorities. Katy's high school days became miserable, and she reported that she frequently went home in tears. Because nothing was done, Katy's brother finally cleaned up the degrading words. Then, when she was out of high school, Katy filed a lawsuit through the Minnesota Department of Human Rights, and in 1991 won a $15,000 settlement against her school.

• In 1992, charges of sexual harassment were brought on behalf of Cheltzie Hentz, a seven-year-old elementary school student in Eden Prairie, Minnesota, who reported being harassed by boys on the school bus. The boys used foul language, joked about body parts, and demanded sexual acts. When Cheltzie told her mother, Sue Mutziger, what was happening to her, Mutziger at first thought her daughter was exaggerating and was going through a time of adjustment. But by the middle of the school year, Cheltzie had become increasingly upset about the daily bus ride, and her mother wanted to know exactly what kinds of things the boys were saying. Mutziger told a reporter that Cheltzie "came out with the foulest, most vulgar, obscene language I could ever imagine, that I hadn't heard till I was twenty years old."[3] Mutziger repeatedly wrote to school authorities asking them to correct the situation, but she was not satisfied with the slow action of the school and decided to file complaints on Cheltzie's behalf with the state and federal governments. The suit was settled in Cheltzie's favor.

• Fifteen-year-old Dianne Triplett of Odessa, Florida, responded to a 1994 *Parade Magazine* inquiry about sexual harassment by describing an incident in seventh grade when "a boy on my bus said nasty, unrepeatable things to me and several times touched my breasts. Now I wish that I had broken his wrist or at least told someone about it. But back then I thought that if I said anything, everyone would get mad at me or make fun of me, because this boy was very popular."[4]

• In Sonoma County, California, a lawsuit was filed in 1994 on behalf of a girl known only as Jane Doe, charging that she was heckled throughout her seventh-grade year and into the next with rumors about her sexual practices—specifically that she had sex with hot dogs. Although Jane Doe's mother complained many times to a counselor about these persistent rumors and the students who were repeating them, school officials reportedly did not inform the harassers' parents or reprimand the harassers. However, lawyers for the school board said that once the school "became aware of the problem, it suspended two boys, had them write letters of apology, and counseled them on why engaging in this kind of behavior is not good."[5]

Controversial Surveys

Along with individual cases, several national surveys in recent years have revealed that sexual harassment of students is a problem nationwide. The Wellesley (Massachusetts) College Center for Research on Women and the NOW Legal Defense and Education Fund developed a survey on sexual harassment that was published in 1993 in *Seventeen* magazine. Nan Stein, who directs the Sexual Harassment in Schools Project at Wellesley, helped analyze a random sampling of the 4,200 responses, reporting that 89 percent of the respondents said they were targets of sexual comments, gestures, or looks; 83 percent reported being touched, pinched, or grabbed; and 39 percent said they had been harassed daily at school.[6]

Perhaps the most frequently quoted survey is one that was conducted in 1993 by Louis Harris and Associates for the American Association of University Women (AAUW). The survey report, called "Hostile Hallways," was based on responses from 1,634 students, eighth through eleventh grade, in seventy-nine schools. Out of that number, 85 percent of the girls and 76 percent of the boys surveyed reported that they had been subjected to unwelcome sexual behavior in classrooms or school corridors. Conduct ranged from sexual insults and leers to clothes being pulled off.

In the opinion of some students, behavior labeled sexual harassment is "no big deal." That has also been an argument used by critics of the AAUW survey and by many others who shrug off unwelcome or crude male behavior by saying "boys will be boys." Touching, grabbing, and pinching are "what young teenage boys do," wrote Jon Margolis, in a *Chicago Tribune* article. "This is not sexual harassment. This is adolescence, a period of life in which immature people discover sex and react with embarrassment, insecurity and a bit of crudeness."[7]

Ken Schroeder, managing editor of *The Education Digest*, also took issue with AAUW's survey, which labeled as sexual harassment such conduct as telling dirty jokes, leaving sexual messages on desks or lockers, "mooning," or intentionally brushing against someone in a sexual way. As Schroeder wrote: "Theoretically, a note saying 'Fuck you!' is sexual, but in the real world, kids seem able to fathom that its message is angry, not sexual." He acknowledged that some adolescent behavior is "immature and meant to embarrass fellow students or to get them to be 'uncool' or whatever the teenage 'un' word is today—but being made to feel awkward does not have any inherently sexual context."[8]

Betsy Hart, a former press secretary to the House Republican Policy Committee, also criticized the AAUW survey in a newspaper column. In her view, boys and girls who take part in sexual types of conduct are simply "teasing and being teased about their sexual maturity, or lack thereof," and the intent of the AAUW "and the feminist sisterhood" is to "teach lots of young people, especially girls, to feel sexually harassed and victimized, both now and later in life."[9]

"Not so," say many others. Indeed, the AAUW used terms and descriptions of sexual harassment in its study that were similar to those used to define sexual harassment in the workplace. And in many instances of harassment on the job—wherever that might be—male harassers often have exhibited behavior learned during adolescence: showing lack of respect for girls and women.

"Sexual harassment causes incredible pain to the victims and it is only now that schools and parents are starting to help," said Robert J. Shoop, consultant for school districts dealing with sexual harassment and author of several popular books on the subject. During a 1994 ten-city book publication tour and appearances at more than sixty national radio call-in shows, Shoop said he heard "pain and anguish" in the voices of many of the callers who had been harassed, which was "really difficult to deal with," but made him even more convinced of the need to address and prevent sexual harassment in schools.[10]

Need for Adult Support

Girls especially need reinforcement when they make complaints about harassment. According to some adults who have dealt with this problem in schools, girls need to know that reporting unwelcome sexual behavior by boys is not a "wimpy" or babyish thing to do. As Ruth Z. Sweetser, a member of the board of directors of the Illinois AAUW, pointed out: "Sexual harassment is not just adolescence or hormones run amok; it can be emotionally painful and academically destructive. . . . Societal norms, such as 'boys will be boys,' must be challenged. By ignoring sexual harassment, we are, in effect, condoning it and enabling its role in the future home and workplace."[11]

One father, a teacher in a rural Iowa town, who had been advised to ignore the sexual harassment of his teenage daughter, decided to do just the opposite, even though he agreed that sometimes adults make things worse and that "in 99 percent of the cases," problems between kids "will work themselves out." He believed, however, that the sexual harassment of his daughter "had gotten out of hand."

Some of the teenager's peers had started a rumor about her—a rumor that could "actually ruin one's reputation"—that circulated for almost the entire

1993–1994 school year. Then, in the spring of 1994, the Iowa teenager "found a sexually explicit note left in her locker by an ex-boyfriend and her ex-best girlfriend." The ex-girlfriend admitted she and the boy had written the note "but said they had thrown it in a trash can and she didn't know who put it in my daughter's locker," the father said.

The father discussed the incident with the school principal, "a former counselor with specialized training in conflict management," who allowed the teenager to confront her harasser under whatever circumstances she felt would be comfortable. According to the father's report, his daughter met with her ex-girlfriend privately and then brought in the principal "once some type of agreement had been reached to 'kind of' formalize things. The meeting was held . . . in the principal's office but nothing appeared to be happening and 'truth' was difficult to come by. Eventually my daughter requested other students come forward to confront the girl."

Although the principal warned the harassers that there would be "serious repercussions" if the harassment did not stop, they received no punishment. Still, the father hoped the warning would have some effect, and he kept "meticulous notes" as evidence. In addition, the father was "very upfront" with the parents of the girl and told them that he would contact a lawyer if necessary. The father reported that the other parents "seemed to understand totally and appeared supportive of my position."[12]

When adults do not attempt to stop unwelcome sexual behavior in schools, they not only teach girls to be passive and suffer silently, but they also send students the message that it's OK to intimidate or assault others. Fear of harassment in turn can discourage or prevent students from attending certain activities or choosing specific classes. In short, as Nan Stein put it: "Sexual harassment may poison the environment, reinforcing the idea that school isn't a safe or a just place."[13]

Betraying a Trust

That concept certainly comes across when teachers, coaches, and other authority figures in schools take advantage of students' vulnerability and emerging awareness of their sexuality. Unfortunately, stories of adult male authority figures abusing their relationships with young girls and betraying their trust appear over and over again in the news. A 1994 syndicated news feature, for one, focused on how school coaches sexually harass athletes, both male and female, but in particular girls who have been taught to see men as powerful authority figures.

Reporter Linda Robertson found that a "small minority of male coaches . . . use their power to twist girls' loyalty into infatuation, then shame." The topic was always discussed whenever female athletic directors got together for meetings, Robertson was told. Every woman that she interviewed for her story "had observed at least one incident of unethical behavior by a male coach or knew someone who had been a victim."

Among the instances that Robertson described was the story of Linda Van Housen, who charged that at the age of thirteen she was sexually molested by her track coach, Michael Ipsen. According to the report, Ipsen, who in 1994 was still a coach in the San Francisco area, convinced the young runner that "submitting to sex with him would prove her devotion." Ipsen also persuaded Van Housen's mother, a recent divorcee, to let the teenager move in with Ipsen and his family so that the girl "would have a father in her life." But Ipsen regularly molested Van Housen, who said she remembered "lying awake in bed at night, listening for the TV to go off and his footsteps at my door, and the numb terror of seeing him walk to my bed." She also said she was once forced to "perform oral sex on him in the car during a road trip to a track meet."[14]

Although Ipsen and his lawyer have consistently denied all the charges, about a dozen other former runners besides Van Housen testified against the coach. Van Housen won a civil lawsuit against Ipsen in 1993, and a jury awarded her $1.1 million in damages.

School Prevention Policies

While Van Housen's case was an extreme example of sexual harassment and abuse of a student by an authority figure, other types of sexual misconduct are increasingly under scrutiny. Courts have found that the school environment is like the work environment in terms of sexual harassment cases that may be filed under federal civil rights laws. Some states—including California, Illinois, Nebraska, Tennessee, and Vermont—also have enacted laws barring sexual harassment in the workplace and schools.

State laws may require that schools have written policies to prevent a hostile and intimidating educational environment. Minnesota, for example, requires schools to post rules about sexual misconduct and the consequences of such behavior and to include those regulations in student handbooks. The state's high school athletic association also has published a policy on sexual harassment, which is included in a booklet on gender equity in school sports.

Whether or not there are state laws in place against sexual harassment in schools, more and more school boards and administrators are beginning to develop and implement sexual harassment policies and procedures. One model for a school sexual harassment policy and complaint procedure was developed by the Northwest Women's Law Center in Seattle, Washington, and it is included in the Appendix at the end of this book.

Susan Strauss, a Minnesota consultant who has designed and directed educational training programs on sexual harassment, also has developed guidelines that some schools have used. They include a statement emphasizing that sexual harassment is illegal, a definition of sexual harassment, examples of specific conduct that is illegal harassment, consequences for students and adults who harass and adult staff who fail to act on harassment charges, and time frames and procedures for filing grievances and making appeals. Suggestions for policies and procedures are spelled out in detail in Strauss's guide *Sexual Harassment and Teens*, published in 1992. Designed for use in grades seven through twelve, the guide has been used as a basis for teaching a course on sexual harassment and by community and youth groups and others interested in preventing such discriminatory behavior.

Schools also have used a guide developed by the Center for Sex Equity in Schools at the University of

Michigan. Called *Tune in to Your Rights: A Guide for Teenagers about Turning Off Sexual Harassment*, the booklet is in the form of a journal and includes questions and answers about various scenarios that could or could not be labeled sexual harassment. Since the booklet's publication in 1985, tens of thousands of copies have been ordered by school personnel, a sign that some schools are making the effort to help students become aware of their legal right to an education free from sexual harassment.

Yet some school personnel say that there is a kind of hysteria going on regarding sexual harassment and sexual abuse allegations. Many male teachers, principals, coaches, directors of recreational programs, and others who work with young people are afraid to show any affection toward students. Although many school personnel still show affection and give appropriate hugs and pats on the back, they tend to be more watchful and careful.

Some schools have adopted a "no-touch" approach for dealing with students, as have various organizations, from the Boy Scouts to religious youth groups. As a result, some educators charge that there is a "big chill" in the schools.

One does not have to be a child psychologist or other behavior expert to know that children need hugs and kisses, pats on the back, and other nurturing touches and attention. "But now, if you mention touch, people think about sexual abuse," according to Cordelia Anderson of Minneapolis, who lectures on sexual health and violence prevention. "Many adults are more worried about litigation and protecting themselves than giving children what they really need," Anderson told an Associated Press reporter.[15]

A male principal of a Midwest elementary school echoed that view. "There was a time when I wouldn't hesitate to pull a crying kid on my lap to comfort him or her. But no more. Today I could be accused of and sued for some type of sexually deviant behavior."[16]

False accusations of that type may be rare, but they are devastating. In the spring of 1994, a substitute teacher in Chicago was falsely accused of molesting eleven fourth-grade students, and school officials and police were ready to believe the accusations. But after much prodding, authorities learned many of the students in the fourth-grade class had been misbehaving and the substitute teacher had threatened to report them. To get even, a student had offered to pay ten other classmates a dollar each if they would claim the teacher molested all of them. The teacher was never charged because the students recanted or changed their stories. But accusations create suspicion, and they can and do damage reputations.

In spite of his ordeal, the teacher said that his case was an exception to the actual incidents of abuse that should be investigated and prosecuted. Many other educators and child advocates insist that the increasing awareness of what constitutes sexual harassment and abuse is necessary in order to make schools and children safer—emotionally and physically.

CHAPTER SIX

Conflicts on Campus

Debates and discussions about sexual issues have been a part of the college scene for years. But the controversy in recent times has centered on such issues as whether or not there is widespread harassment of students by professors or others in authority positions on college campuses. Ellen A. Paludi, an expert on the subject who was interviewed for a 1994 issue of *Money* magazine, reported: "Research, including my own, suggests that about 30 percent of female students will come under pressure for sexual favors from professors or instructors. If you include other types of harassment, such as sexist or demeaning comments by professors about students' bodies, the figure rises to 85 percent. Male students are harassed too, almost always by male professors, but the incidence is much lower."[1]

Related issues question whether universities and colleges should ban professors from dating students and whether sexual harassment charges make women appear more like helpless victims than strong, independent people. There also have been arguments over what constitutes date rape and whether feminist politics prevents legitimate debate on sexual issues.

Politically Incorrect Behavior or Illegal Harassment?

Some of the debates seem to get bogged down in arguments over what is considered appropriate, or "politically correct" (PC), behavior and language. At one college, for example, an English professor insisted that she was sexually harassed (made to feel "uncomfortable" and therefore unable to do her work) because a reproduction of a famous painting of a nude woman by Francisco Goya was hanging in her classroom; the painting was removed and placed in the student-center reading room.

Charges of sexual harassment also have been made because of classroom statements or discussions that some students have considered offensive. At Los Angeles Valley College, students accused a teacher of sexual harassment after he reportedly joked that they would have to do the work assigned because he did not accept credit cards, checks, or sexual favors.

One widely publicized report in the spring of 1994 focused on a religion scholar, Graydon Snyder, who had been teaching at the Chicago Theological Seminary for more than three decades. In his classes, Snyder compared the Jewish Talmud with Protestant scriptures, using a story to raise a hypothetical question about whether sin is intended. The story, often told by rabbis, is about a workman who falls from a roof, landing on a woman and apparently having sexual contact with her. Because the workman did not intend such an act, it did not constitute "degradation," as the contact would otherwise be called.

When a female student complained that this story was offensive, seminary officials placed Snyder on probation and ordered him to apologize to the student. In May 1994, Snyder filed a lawsuit against the seminary, charging defamation of character. Other biblical scholars supported his cause; they feared that biblical literature would be censored by students who didn't like the numerous and varied sexual references and interpreted them according to their own prejudices.

Different interpretations of what constitutes sexual harassment are the essence of some cases that are based on "he said, she said" arguments. News stories for months in the fall of 1993, for instance, covered an exchange between two first-year students at Swarthmore College in Pennsylvania: Alexis Clinansmith, an eighteen-year-old from an upscale suburban Michigan community, and Ewart Yearwood, an eighteen-year-old from Spanish Harlem in New York City.

Clinansmith accused Yearwood of unwelcome romantic overtures, saying he waited for her outside classrooms, followed her to dances, football games, and lectures, and used vulgar language. Yearwood faced suspension, but in a letter to the college president, he disputed the charges and stated that Clinansmith had never indicated to him that she felt intimidated by his behavior. He felt she was reacting to the fact that he came from a tough neighborhood and was an athlete with a shaved head who looked "mean."

The Dean's Committee heard the case and could not agree on whether Yearwood should be suspended; the committee ordered Yearwood to stay away from Clinansmith and eventually decided to drop the sexual harassment charges against him if he agreed to attend another college for a semester. But that decision created even more controversy when Yearwood was rejected by Columbia, the college he chose as a substitute. Although he enrolled at Boston University in January 1994, in the end there was no clear decision on whether or not sexual harassment took place.

In spite of the fine line—or wavy gray line, as some call it—that at times seems to divide what is sexual harassment and what is not, there is little doubt that distinct incidents of sexual harassment have taken place on college campuses, including public, private, and military institutions. As the superintendent of the Air Force Academy at Colorado Springs, Colorado, pointed out when he initiated a 1994 crackdown on sexual harassment: "We didn't realize the extent" of the work that has to be done.[2]

Date Rape Charges

Some groups of women on college campuses believe that there is also a great deal of work to be done to prevent sexual assault and "date rape," or sexual intercourse without mutual consent. Of course, sexual assault, like sexual harassment, is illegal, but the issue of what constitutes date rape has generated as much debate as that of sexual harassment.

On one side are individuals and groups who argue that, if there is sexual contact, a girl or woman should be able to consent to every move because females have less power than males and may otherwise be forced into sex against their will when they are on a date or with a male acquaintance or friend. Such groups support guides or codes detailing consensual behavior—for example, obtaining permission to kiss or to touch. Consent must be sober as well, since someone who has been drinking alcoholic beverages or ingesting other types of drugs is not in control and able to give rational consent.

In 1993, male and female students at Antioch College in Ohio established specific guidelines for consensual sex. The guidelines prompted some public ridicule because the list of "may I do this" or "may I do that" questions made them read rather like a sex manual. But the guidelines were serious: A student who violated the code or had sex with someone who was unable to give consent faced expulsion. Numerous other colleges and universities have also set up codes and penalties (although not quite as strict as Antioch's) for sexual behavior on campus. In addition, some schools conduct seminars and publish pamphlets on date rape and how to prevent it.

At the same time, activist groups on campuses across the United States have held "Take Back the Night!" rallies to protest violence on campus. In some instances, the names of those who have been accused of sexual assault have been scrawled on sidewalks or have been posted on bulletin boards. And countless discussions have focused on how to avoid rape on campus.

Critics say that so-called feminist activities have created fear and defensive attitudes among women on campus. Some have complained that those who campaign against date rape and sexual harassment on campus will deny men their "privilege" of aggression and initiative. Some have even declared that male impotence will be the result of the feminist campaign.

And one Canadian professor wrote in a student news-paper that date rape was necessary because young men require regular sexual intercourse. (The professor was suspended, and the university president declared in an editorial that date rape was never acceptable.)

Katie Roiphe, in a controversial book, *The Morning After: Sex, Fear, and Feminism on Campus*, claims that "rape-crisis feminists" have created unnecessary trauma and are trying to regulate sex, dictating the way it should or should not be. Roiphe did not include interviews with rape victims and used statistics from only one authority, who has long asserted that date rape is not as common as many people believe. Nevertheless, she concluded that women are becoming wimpy victims rather than learning to enjoy free love. Roiphe argues that "rules and laws based on the premise that all women need protection from all men, because they are so much weaker, serve only to reinforce the image of women as powerless."[3]

Others have echoed this concept, often discounting reports of sexual violence on campus or elsewhere and calling prevention advocates "neo-Victorian prudes." According to Mary Matalin, cohost of the TV talk show "Equal Time," sexual harassment policies are based "on the overhyped problem of campus date rape" and "the man-hating extremist notion that all heterosexual males are testosterone-mad, uncontrollable rapists."[4]

In an opinion piece for the *Los Angeles Times*, Judith Sherven, a clinical psychologist in West Los Angeles, wrote: "Sexual harassment cannot ever be eradicated because much of it exists through the interpretive eye of the beholder. Confusion and miscommunication between men and women is a reality to be learned about and negotiated rather than wished away." Sherven further stated:

> Radical feminist rhetoric . . . undermines the goal of equal rights and responsibilities for women in favor of the romantic and narcissistic ideal of a perfect, stress-free world—for women. In this disempowering fantasy, women do not have to grow up or become responsible for themselves. That leaves men the only responsible people on the planet. Instead of insisting that women achieve their potential, the makers of these child's-world fantasies encourage women to blame men and society for all of their difficulties.[5]

Those who take a middle road on these issues agree that sexual harassment can never be eliminated entirely. But as Andi Ackerman of Los Angeles wrote in a rebuttal to Sherven's arguments:

> Does [Sherven] truly believe that employees or students, male or female, whose job security or academic grade are tied to their willingness to endure sexually explicit requests, compliments and outright sexual encounters to be romantic, narcissistic whiners if they are not empowered by their dehumanizing reality, and that they are "dependent" and "squeamish" to raise their voices in protest? Does she believe that to want something better, that to strive to improve an injustice, is disempowering? If one were to follow that line of thought, then Martin Luther King's dream is a whiny fantasy.[6]

Some middle-of-the-roaders also say that in certain cases sexual rules and regulations may go too far and eventually be a threat to basic freedoms. But they do not want to continue the abuses of power that keep women subordinate economically and socially or to dismantle laws that provide protection against physical coercion. The fact is, in the real world, in spite of great gains by some women, most have not achieved equity and do not have the authority or financial means needed to fight back.

Faculty-Student Relationships

Another major debate on campus has been over the question, Should a member of the faculty be romantically involved with a student? Or, is it ethical for an instructor and a student to engage in a sexual relationship?

The issue certainly is not new, according to an account written by a twelfth-century French philosopher, Peter Abelard, who tutored a young student named Héloïse and became sexually involved with her. Héloïse's doting uncle had entrusted Abelard with the education of his niece. But with ample privacy and "with our lessons as a pretext we abandoned ourselves entirely to love. . . . Our desires left no stage of lovemaking untried," Abelard wrote.[7] The couple married, but when their affair was discovered, there was a public outcry that led to Abelard's castration for betraying a trust, and both entered monasteries, he as a monk, and she as a nun.

Today's public controversy stems, in part, from the view that teachers, like other professionals in authority positions, should support and encourage but not become sexually intimate with those they mentor. There is also concern that a relationship between a professor and a student may be coerced, even though both are consenting adults. In other words, students (usually young, vulnerable women) may be naively awed and enticed into sexual unions, believing they are "in love," or they may be pressured to provide sexual favors for male professors or teaching assistants in exchange for grades or for scholarships or other educational benefits.

Professors have the power to determine the fate of students, so if they abuse that power in a sexual manner, students usually remain silent. That was the case of a student who wrote to Deborah Taylor, founder of a student sexual harassment committee at State University of New York at Cortland. Taylor received a letter from a student who had been harassed but did not speak out because she feared retaliatory measures. The sexual harasser "or some of his allies might be on some scholarship committees and would have lessened or ruined my chances of being awarded those scholarships," the student wrote. "And as I come from a poor, working-class background, I had absolutely no financial support from my relatives. I wouldn't have been able to continue my studies if I hadn't won those scholarships. The very idea of being denied my financial security, and therefore my education, scared me silent."[8]

Two other students that Taylor talked to had been harassed by the chair of their department but would not file formal charges because they were "worried about their degrees." The harasser could determine grades and even whether they would graduate.

Because of the potential for abuse, some in academia say that professors or other educators in authority positions should *never* date or have sexual relationships with any students. As one feminist scholar at the University of Illinois at Chicago pointed out in an electronic conference on the topic:

> It is wrong from the perspective of sisterhood for a nubile young attractive student to compete with a wife, usually with children, who has seen the professor when he was a grungy graduate student and doesn't write down every word he says. . . . It is particularly wrong when the man is in a position of power over you. It makes the transaction much like prostitution.[9]

Others say faculty-student liaisons should be discouraged in situations where an instructor is teaching or supervising a student, but they do not advocate an outright ban, citing the right to privacy and the belief that college students are adults and responsible for their own decisions. Still others adamantly oppose any type of restrictions on relationships between faculty and students and say that it is patronizing for others to determine who an individual should date or with whom a person should develop a friendship.

Barry M. Dank, professor of sociology, California State University, Long Beach, founded and is the director of an organization known as Consenting Academics for Sexual Equity (CASE). He and others who are part of the group "feel that men and women in different organizational power positions need not be in abusive relationships. We believe that attempting to ban love/sexual relationships between persons of different social categories is a form of tyranny, and must be overtly opposed." Dank charged that those who would ban professor-student relationships have "unfairly and inaccurately" portrayed male professors as "lechers" and stereotyped female students "as helpless fragile victims who need protection. It propels such women back into the traditional category of 'women and children.' We vehemently protest and oppose those who attempt to take away from adult women the right of consent. Female university students are not children!"

The organization's statement of principles declares:

> CASE rejects the concept that consenting adult sexual relationships can fall under the rubric of sexual harassment. Sexual harassment cannot occur unless there is unwanted sexual attention. CASE regards the attempts of universities to regulate the behavior of consenting academics as a form of sexual harassment in itself. In this regard, we are also concerned that such banning policies may also be employed as a guise to regulate or ban other forms of consensual adult relationships, such as interracial, inter-age, and same sex relationships. Our concern also includes the effects of academic banning on all kinds of academic relationships, such as non-sexual friendships and mentoring relationships.[10]

While agreeing with some of the principles of CASE, other academics argue that even though some students are legally adults, their behavior on campus (and in society at large) is restricted in a variety of ways, such as not being allowed to bring cars on campus, to drink or smoke in university buildings, or, in some cases, to live off campus.

Summing up such a view, Martin Schwartz, a sociologist at Ohio University, put it this way:

> No culture on the face of the earth has ever allowed all members unlimited sexual access to all other members. All have rules, and virtually all feel that some sexual relations "foul the nest," even between consenting adults. . . . I quite understand the right people claim to use their bodies in any way they wish. However, we have never agreed as a society to that principle. You are not allowed to legally be a crack addict on most campuses; you cannot go to a bar after closing hours; you cannot have sex in the middle of the street, whether alone or with others; you cannot be publicly intoxicated, and, in many places, you cannot smoke a cigarette indoors. There are lots of restrictions on what you can do with your body.[11]

But the questions still remain: Is there a conflict of interest when a faculty member is romantically involved with a student? Won't that student have an unfair advantage over others? Is it possible to objectively evaluate a student when there are romantic ties? When a relationship goes awry, will a professor or student seek revenge? Should students expect to be protected from faculty who exploit in a sexual manner? Can a university legally ban faculty-student relationships? Is that an infringement of a basic right to exercise one's free will?

Policies and Penalties

At Syracuse University (SU) in New York State, officials developed a policy statement in 1993 that underscores the university's commitment "to maintaining a research, learning, living, and work environment free of sexual harassment," using educational programs primarily but also disciplinary measures. Like other universities and colleges with sexual harassment policies, SU defined sexual harassment, outlined the federal and state laws regarding such behavior, and presented the methods for making complaints and seeking remedial action. The policy also emphasized the imbalances and dangers that are inherent in amorous relationships "between any teacher, supervisor, or officer of the University and any person for whom he or she has a professional responsibility." As the policy states:

> Professionalism within the University demands that those with authority not abuse, nor seem to abuse, the power with which they are entrusted. Administrators, supervisors, faculty members and graduate assistants of the University thus need to hold themselves to a high professional standard and avoid intimacy with the students and

subordinates with whom they work, recognizing that such relationships pose a professional conflict of interest that may make it difficult, if not impossible, to carry out their role as educators. It is thus the responsibility of all individuals who are involved in an amorous relationship with a person whose work they supervise to take whatever steps are needed to avoid a conflict of interest. This may include reporting the relationship to an appropriate supervisor, who can then monitor the individual's grading or other evaluation for possible bias or perception of bias by others who may be aware of the relationship.[12]

Similar statements have been included in the policies or ethics codes of other universities. At the University of California at Berkeley, for example, the code of ethics does not ban faculty-student alliances, but it does clearly label such relationships as "unprofessional." A policy statement at the University of Chicago declares, "Prudence and the best interest of the students dictates that, in such circumstances of romantic involvement, the students should be aided to find other instructional or supervisory arrangements."[13]

"It is a violation of University policy" at Tufts if a faculty member becomes involved in "an amorous, dating, or sexual relationship with a student whom he/she instructs, evaluates, supervises, advises." The Tufts University policy calls student consent to such a relationship "suspect." That term is also applied at Indiana University, where a faculty-student relationship is "unacceptable" if "the faculty member has professional responsibility for the student."[14]

All romantic relationships between faculty and students were outlawed at the University of Kansas in the summer of 1993. The policy came about because of a law school professor who sexually harassed a student and was later fired.

Suspension, firing, or forced resignation is frequently the consequence when faculty or others in authority breach university policies on sexual discrimination and harassment. In the spring of 1994 the University of Pennsylvania called for the resignation of Malcolm Woodfield, assistant professor of English. According to a press release from the university, Woodfield "admitted that he engaged in sexual relations with a student in his class and that this was unethical under the University's policies. Professor Woodfield regrets his behavior and, by resigning, takes full responsibility for it," the university's announcement declared, adding:

> The University of Pennsylvania takes very seriously its ethical responsibilities to its students. No nonacademic or personal ties should be allowed to interfere with the academic integrity of the teacher-student relationship. In accordance with its policies and practice, the University deals vigorously and decisively with any complaints that might arise of unethical and inappropriate behavior.[15]

CHAPTER SEVEN

Preventing Discrimination and Harassment

Whatever the policies and punishments established in an effort to prevent sexual harassment in schools and the workplace, rules and regulations alone won't solve the problem. Many educational consultants, social science researchers, and others say that prevention also requires other strategies. One is tackling a closely related issue: gender equity in educational institutions. Another is educating the public about gender bias and creating broader public awareness of gender discrimination and sexual harassment in schools as well as in the workplace.

Educational inequities place girls and women at a disadvantage and set the stage for stereotypes—assumptions about what girls and women cannot or should not do—which lead to treating women as ignorant, weak, passive, and subordinate. That in turn contributes to job discrimination based on gender and blatant sexual harassment on the job and in schools.

The AAUW Report

Although the U.S. Congress in 1972 outlawed discrimination based on gender in public schools, numerous studies and surveys show that girls and women seldom receive an education equal to that of boys and men. Just as girls and boys are socialized differently, so girls and boys are taught differently in schools. That was the conclusion of a landmark report, *How Schools Shortchange Girls*, written by the Center for Research on Women at Wellesley College and released in 1992 by the American Association of University Women (AAUW).

Among the findings, the AAUW report stated that girls in the early grades usually achieve as well as or better than boys, but girls fall behind in later years because of subtle biases that can foster lower educational expectations than those for boys and men. Classmates often harass girls who appear to be "too smart," and boys, who make up the majority of advanced science and math classes, belittle girls who try to participate. In many other educational activities, such as school sports, girls often get the message that they "aren't as good" as boys, and eventually may lose confidence in themselves and end up with low self-esteem. According to the AAUW, a study of three thousand children ages nine to fifteen showed that 60 percent of elementary school girls and 69 percent of elementary school boys were "happy the way I am" but by high school only 29 percent of the girls reported high self-esteem compared with 46 percent of boys.

Some other conclusions that have been widely publicized include the following:

• Because boys in general are more aggressive in the classroom than girls, teachers (often without intent) are more likely to call on boys for response to a question rather than encourage girls to give an answer or opinion.

• Even if they do well in scientific or technological studies, girls are generally not encouraged to take advanced math and science courses or computer classes in school; in many instances such courses are still considered "boys' subjects."

• Although there are many nonsexist educational materials, teachers may use older textbooks and curriculum materials that include images of males and females in stereotypical roles, reinforcing the notion that people are expected to behave in gender-specific ways.

• Teachers frequently encourage boys to solve problems on their own, while offering more assistance to girls in problem solving, fostering "learned helplessness," as researchers call it, and discouraging perseverance in education.

Yet there are critics of the study, among them Christina Hoff Sommers, a professor of philosophy at Clark University, in Worcester, Massachusetts, who examined the data on which the conclusions were based. In Sommers's view, the findings were flawed, in part because of the types of questions asked, such as those used to determine and compare adolescent girls' and boys' self-esteem.

As Sommers noted in a July 1994 opinion piece for *The Washington Post*, "the AAUW counted as 'unhappy' all respondents who had checked 'sort of true,' and 'sometimes true/sometimes false.' If one rejects that bizarre approach, the percentage of unhappy girls is dramatically lower: 12 percent, not 71 percent, as the study indicates." According to Sommers:

The AAUW also failed to publicize the very awkward finding that African-American boys, who are educationally most at risk, score highest of all on the AAUW's self-esteem indexes: 78 percent of African-American boys said they were "always" "happy the way I am" compared with 34 percent of white girls. Black girls too are well ahead of white girls as well as white boys on the self-esteem scale. These results undermine either the link the AAUW claims between self-esteem and academic performance or the study's controversial methodology of measuring "self-esteem" by polling children for "happiness" responses.[1]

The Gender Equity in Education Act

Whatever flaws there might be in the AAUW report, it spurred the U.S. Congressional Caucus for Women's Issues to propose a bill in 1993 known as the Gender Equity in Education Act, intended to remedy some of the gender bias problems in schools. Congresswoman Patsy T. Mink of Hawaii, cosponsor of the bill, said the bill was "a collection of nine proposals developed by individual members of the Caucus" that "includes initiatives to combat sexual harassment in schools, provide teacher training on equity issues, improve girls' achievement in math and science, . . . address inequities in athletic programs, and improve data collection." To coordinate the programs, the bill also provided for an office of gender equity within the U.S. Department of Education.

In announcing the legislative package, Mink said, "The only way for women to achieve parity with their male colleagues in a highly technical, high-skilled workforce is to assure that they have the same opportunities and encouragement beginning at the earliest level of education and continuing through higher education."[2]

The Gender Equity Act, which was integrated into the Elementary and Secondary Education Act, passed in late December 1994. The Act provides funds for programs designed to counter gender bias in education. But even before the law passed, some school systems, professional groups, and activist organizations had launched campaigns on their own.

Programs to Eliminate Gender Bias

The American Association for the Advancement of Science (AAAS), for instance, established a program in 1989 called Girls in Science: Linkages for the Future that trains leaders (women) of Girl Scout Councils to do hands-on science and math activities. In turn, the women show local Girl Scout leaders how to conduct the programs for their troops.

Abbott Laboratories, a major pharmaceutical firm based in northern Illinois, sponsored such a training program in 1993, in part because the company is well aware that there will be an estimated shortage of 675,000 engineers and scientists by 2010. To reduce that shortage, many more women will have to enter scientific fields. But that won't happen unless there are more role models and mentors for girls, which the AAAS program also attempts to provide, calling on professional women in science to meet and talk with trainees and encourage more support—at home and at school—for girls interested in science. As many gender-equity experts have noted, counseling in school can help, but parents also play a key role in girls' expectations. If, for example, a mother constantly asserts that she is "dumb at math," she is not likely to instill confidence in a daughter who might be trying to gain skills in the field.

A Computer Expert Equity Project (CEEP) funded by the National Science Foundation and seven major corporations teaches educators in all fifty states to become trainers for teachers in their local areas, showing them how to identify and reduce gender bias not only in science and math courses but also in related training for computer technology.

According to educators, boys and girls start out in early childhood with an equal interest in computers, but in the middle grades girls begin to drop out of computer classes. Why? The reasons are similar to those described in the AAUW report. When it comes to elective courses, boys dominate the computer room and after-school computer club, and at home the computer often is used primarily by the boys or men in the household. As a result, girls get the idea that making computers function is rather like making car engines run—a traditional male interest.

Male dominance is also apparent in computer science—men who earn degrees in the field outnumber women three to one, according to the National Science Foundation, which expects the gap to widen in the years ahead.[3] Computer sales, computer games (which are often shoot-'em-up types), and even the Internet, a global communication and resource network, and commercial network services such as CompuServe, Prodigy, and America Online are chiefly male-oriented. On forums and listservs (electronic mailing lists) men frequently take over "conversations" and sometimes become hostile or violently argumentative (a practice called "flaming"). Kimberly Cook, a sociologist at the University of New Hampshire, the founder of Sociologists Against Sexual Harassment and a member of its electronic network (SASH-L), warned subscribers after one heated exchange: " 'One-up-manship' may be the theme and tone of the day on other electronic lists; but let's not sink to that level."[4]

Men and boys on electronic networks may also sexually harass women and girls, making blatant sexual advances through electronic mail (E-mail). These practices can turn females against computer use, although to avoid harassment women have begun setting up their own forums and listservs.

In spite of the various obstacles, Jo Sanders, director of CEEP, which is based at the City University of New York, is convinced that there is progress in reducing gender bias in many areas of computer technology. She has found that CEEP trainers have been making an impact, helping computer science teachers bring more female students into computer classes and activities. The teachers use strategies such as emphasizing cooperative learning, which appeals to many girls, and having more female aides in computer classes.

Teachers also concentrate on projects that interest both girls and boys. As a teacher of a computer programming course in an Alexandria, Virginia, school explained: "Boys like to play games where they are challenged to get the highest score they can; girls like to do things that accomplish an end product."[5]

In other efforts, school administrators bring in consultants to help develop awareness of gender bias within schools and workplaces. One consultant, James Knight, a former professor at Ohio State University, once believed that women and girls should be confined to their traditional roles. But Knight now insists that "you can't have excellence without equity." He left his teaching position in 1988 to become a full-time consultant on communication, teaching, and motivation, and the need to achieve gender equity in schools and the workplace.

In talks to students and teachers at a northern Indiana Career Center, Knight emphasized, "There is no such thing as men's work and women's work. There's just work." He also stressed that "equity is not about women being welders; it's about career choices and who gets to make them." He urged students making nontraditional career choices to seek support from groups and individuals working to reduce gender bias, since it is never easy to go against cultural norms.[6]

One of the most controversial strategies to help girls pursue interests in science, math, and other technical subjects is encouraging them to enroll in private all-girl schools or all-girl classes in public schools. "Although not everyone agrees, most studies show that girls in single-sex schools achieve more, have higher self-esteem and are more interested in subjects like math and science," according to two well-known gender-equity consultants, Myra and David Sadker, both professors of education at American University in Washington, D.C. The Sadkers, who conducted a three-year study of fourth-, sixth-, and eighth-grade classes in four states as well as in the capital, also have found that girls in experimental, single-sex classes in public schools have improved their performance. Girls in such classes appear to participate more and are more assertive and enthusiastic about their studies than those in coed classes.[7]

But, as the Sadkers point out, "Legally, single-sex education in public schools is a sticky business. Laws like Title IX prohibit sex discrimination in public schools, including teaching girls and boys separately in most cases." There are exceptions for laboratory schools, but even so, "Many educators have reservations that go beyond legal problems," calling all-girl classes a "defeatist approach, one that gives up on girls and boys learning equally, side by side. Other critics say that the model focuses on 'fixing up the girls' but leaves boys in the dust," the Sadkers report. They add that most public schools are committed to coeducation, but "educators are becoming convinced that changes need to be made" in the way girls are taught.[8]

At the same time, schools and workplaces are also making many efforts to reduce sexual harassment, as more and more individuals ask: "What should I do if I think I've been discriminated against or harassed?" Or "How do I know if I'm discriminating against or harassing someone?"

Nearly every program, course, seminar, workshop, or set of guidelines and procedures on sexual discrimination and harassment attempts to answer those questions. Although it's impossible to provide responses and advice that will fit each and every situation, some basic suggestions for stopping sexual discrimination and harassment are included on the following pages.

CHAPTER EIGHT

Stopping
Sexual Harassment

One of the first steps an individual can take to stop discriminatory and sexually harassing behavior is to review statements explaining or defining these types of conduct. Sex discrimination includes:

- Rewarding, promoting, or punishing a person on the basis of the recipient's gender rather than performance
- Treating people unequally on the basis of gender in work-related or school-related programs and activities
- Failing to provide female students with the same academic opportunities as male students, or vice versa
- Using classroom materials that ignore or depreciate a group based on gender
- Ignoring an employee's or student's career and educational goals because of the assumption that the goals are inappropriate for the person's gender

Sexual harassment is a form of sex discrimination, and if you have been subjected to illegal sexual harassment in the school or workplace, you will need to identify the specific type(s) of behavior. Examples of sexually harassing behaviors that have been listed in various policy manuals and other publications include:

- Attempted sexual assault or rape
- Unwanted and unwelcome physical contact, such as touching, fondling, or groping
- Invasion of "personal space" by cornering, blocking, or standing too close
- Continued or repeated chatter of a sexual nature and graphic comments about sex
- Offensive and persistent sexual jokes or sexual teasing
- Questions or comments about the sexual activities of your friend or spouse, or about your own sexual preferences
- Sexually suggestive comments, such as "You must be feeling bad because you didn't get enough (sex)" or "A little tender loving care (TLC) will cure your ailments"
- Leers and stares
- Lewd gestures (holding or eating fruit in a deliberate sexual manner) or touching oneself in a sexual manner while in public
- Suggestive noises or sounds such as wolf calls, kissing sounds, or lip smacking
- Offensive sexual pictures, cartoons, and graphics that are posted in a workplace
- Annoying or degrading comments about your body

- Continued pressure to engage in sexual activity
- Threats or suggestions that grades, scholarships, a degree, a job, working conditions, or a promotion depend on your submission to sexual demands

A person who has been accused of harassment has the right to an unbiased investigation and a chance to explain his or her actions. In some cases, an accused person may not realize that certain behaviors are harassment. Unwelcome behavior may stop if the person responsible for it learns how his or her actions affect others. Unfortunately, there are also instances when someone is falsely accused of harassment because the person making the accusation seeks some sort of revenge or simply wants to cause trouble.

Filing a Complaint

If you experience actual and persistent incidents of harassment, keep a detailed journal of the offensive behavior. Talk to a trusted person at school, on the job, or at home, and find advocates who will support you should you decide to make an informal or formal complaint. Remember that unwanted sexual attention *is not your fault*. It is illegal, and you have the right to protection.

Procedures for filing complaints vary with schools and workplaces, but most have written policies against sexual discrimination and harassment and information about whom to contact if complaints are necessary. Depending on the circumstances, formal charges could be filed with the Office for Civil Rights within the U.S. Department of Education; a state human rights commission; a regional or state EEOC office; a state fair-employment practices agency; a local agency that provides protection against sexual harassment under city or county ordinances; a university legal department or office of human relations; or a human rights officer in a public school system.

In some cases, it is necessary to file a private lawsuit; but that can be an expensive option unless an attorney is willing to work on a contingency basis, accepting fees that the court awards or taking a percentage of a court-ordered monetary settlement. There are agencies, organizations, and groups that not only can help locate a lawyer with expertise in sexual harassment cases but also can provide other advice, suggestions, and guidelines for stopping unwanted sexual attention. Some of those resources are listed on pages 123–124.

In the end, as most sexual harassment policies state, you cannot expect discriminatory behavior that disrupts your education or job performance to go away by itself. If you want a situation to change, you have to act, enlisting the support of others whenever possible.

Sometimes there is a high price to pay for speaking out, making formal complaints, or filing lawsuits. You could become the target of retaliation, which in itself could be discriminatory and illegal. But the alternative—remaining silent and doing nothing—may exact an even higher price in terms of an inadequate education, lack of self-respect, poor job performance, stress, and other harmful effects.

Finally, there will always be bullies, oafs, boors, jerks—all-around crude folks—who want to make life miserable for others. And, unfortunately, there will always be people who behave in violent ways. In addition, there are many in society who believe that the "battle of the sexes" is inevitable and that women and men, boys and girls will never be able to bridge the gender gap.

Nevertheless, individuals *are* learning—often through seminars and workshops on sexual discrimination and harassment—that men and women can respect and understand each other. As one high school student concluded after taking part in a sexual harassment prevention program: "Harassment is basic disrespect—so who needs it?"[1]

Source Notes

Chapter One

1. Elizabeth Kadetsky, "The Million-Dollar Man," *Working Woman*, October 1993, p. 52.
2. Dara A. Charney, M.D., and Ruth C. Russell, M.D., "An Overview of Sexual Harassment," *American Journal of Psychiatry*, January 1994, p. 10.
3. Personal correspondence and interview.
4. Mica Glod, "Sexual Harassment: Here at STC?" *X-Ray* (St. Charles [Ill.] High School), April 16, 1993, p. 1.
5. Joan Kelly Bernard, "When Women Sexually Harass Men at Work," *Philadelphia Inquirer*, February 22, 1994, p. C5.
6. Ibid.
7. Kara Swisher, "Laying Down the Law on Harassment," *The Washington Post*, February 6, 1994, p. H1.

Chapter Two

1. William Petrocelli and Barbara Kate Repa, *Sexual Harassment on the Job* (Berkeley, Calif.: Nolo Press, 1992), p. 8/8.

2. Ellen Bravo and Ellen Cassedy, *The 9to5 Guide to Combating Sexual Harassment* (New York: Wiley, 1992), p. 3.
3. Quoted in Kara Swisher, "Laying Down the Law on Harassment," *The Washington Post*, February 6, 1994, p. H1.
4. Barbara Smith, "Ain't Gonna Let Nobody Turn Me Around," *Ms.*, January/February 1992, p. 38.
5. Eleanor Holmes Norton, "And the Language Is Race," *Ms.*, January/February 1992, p. 44.
6. "Sisters in Defense of Professor Hill," advertisement, *The New York Times*, November 17, 1991.
7. Linda Bird Francke, "Paula Coughlin: The Woman Who Changed the U.S. Navy," *Glamour*, June 1993, pp. 159–161, 217–220.
8. Department of Defense, *Tailhook 91, Part 1—Review of the Navy Investigations September 1992* (electronic version).
9. "Indecent Exposure," *Time*, May 3, 1993, pp. 20–21.
10. "Continuing Outrage of Tailhook," Editorial, *Los Angeles Times*, February 12, 1994, p. B7.

Chapter Three

1. Associated Press, "Pepsi Worker Wins Sex Harassment Case," *Chicago Tribune*, February 19, 1994, p. 18.
2. Center for the American Woman and Politics, Fact Sheet, November 1993.
3. Ellen Lewis, "Hers: Making a Difference," *The New York Times Magazine*, December 12, 1993, pp. 50–51.
4. Personal interview, March 10, 1994.
5. Quoted in Shearlean Duke, "A-Plus 'Sexual Hasslement,' " *Los Angeles Times*, February 11, 1993, p. E2.
6. Personal interview, July 15, 1992.
7. Personal interview, July 15, 1992.
8. Elizabeth Kuster, "Don't 'Hey, Baby' Me," *Glamour*, September 1992, pp. 308–311, 332–333.
9. "Beauty, Sports, and Power Feminism," Interview, *Women's Sports & Fitness*, March 1994, p. 24.
10. Quoted in Debra A. Applegate, "Films Put Low Price on Women," *South Bend Tribune*, p. E1.

Chapter Four

1. Anne B. Fisher, "Sexual Harassment—What to Do," *Fortune*, August 23, 1993, pp. 84–85.
2. Diana Kunde, "High Cost of Sexual Harassment in Texas," *Dallas Morning News*, February 21, 1993, p. H1.
3. Andrea Sachs, " '9-Zip! I Love It!' " *Time*, November 22, 1993, p. 44.
4. Northwest Women's Law Center, *Sexual Harassment in Employment and Education* (Seattle: Northwest Women's Law Center, 1992), p. 11.
5. John O'Brien, "Agent Tells of Fear in Sex Harassment Case," *Chicago Tribune*, July 28, 1993, p. 6.
6. Jim Newton, "Sexual Harassment a Tough LAPD Problem," *Los Angeles Times*, March 3, 1994, p. A1.
7. Bill Romano and Jeff Gottlieb, "Suit Alleges Sexual Harassment," *San Jose Mercury News*, May 4, 1994, p. 1B; Donna Alvarado, "Surgeon Renews Bias Battle," *San Jose Mercury News*, February 23, 1994, p. 1B.
8. Miriam Komaromy, Andrew B. Bindman, Richard J. Haber, and Merle A. Sande, "Sexual Harassment in Medical Training," *New England Journal of Medicine*, February 4, 1993, p. 322.
9. Susan P. Phillips and Margaret S. Schneider, *New England Journal of Medicine*, December 23, 1993, p. 1936.
10. *Ellison v. Brady*, 942 F.2d 872 (Ninth Circuit, 1991). Also quoted in William Petrocelli and Barbara Kate Repa, *Sexual Harassment on the Job* (Berkeley, Calif.: Nolo Press, 1992), p. 2/16; and in Ellen Bravo and Ellen Cassedy, *The 9to5 Guide to Combating Sexual Harassment* (New York: Wiley, 1992), p. 32.
11. Bob Levey, "Bob Levey's Washington," *The Washington Post*, March 10, 1994, p. B20.
12. Ellen Bravo and Ellen Cassedy, *The 9to5 Guide to Combating Sexual Harassment* (New York: John Wiley & Sons, 1992), p. 26.
13. "Employer's Prompt Action on Charges Bars Liability for Sexual Harassment," *BNA Corporate Counsel Daily*, December 29, 1993, electronic file.

14. Dara A. Charney, M.D., and Ruth C. Russell, M.D., "An Overview of Sexual Harassment," *American Journal of Psychiatry*, January 1994, p. 10.
15. Quoted in "Sexual Harassment Claim Handling Faulty at Law Enforcement Agencies," *BNA Employment Policy & Law Daily*, March 10, 1994, electronic file.
16. Rinni Sandroff, "Sexual Harassment," *Working Woman*, June 1992, p. 51.
17. Brian S. Baigrie, SASH-L (listserv) electronic posting, February 18, 1994.
18. Quoted in "Cuomo Releases Report," *BNA Employment Policy & Law Daily*, January 27, 1994, electronic file.

Chapter Five

1. Tamar Lewin, "Students' Harassment Suits Near Trial," *Oregonian*, July 24, 1994, p. A16.
2. Quoted in Elizabeth Levitan Spaid, "Schools Grapple with Peer Harassment," *Christian Science Monitor*, January 21, 1993, p. 3.
3. Quoted in Margaret Lillard, Associated Press, "Boys Will be Boys?" *Elkart Truth*, May 31, 1993, p. A1.
4. Quoted in Lynn Minton, "Fresh Voices" column, *Parade Magazine*, February 20, 1994, p. 30.
5. Tamar Lewin, "Students' Harassment Suits Near Trial," *Oregonian*, July 24, 1994, p. A16.
6. Nan Stein, "Stop Sexual Harassment in Schools," *USA Today*, May 18, 1993, p. A11.
7. Jon Margolis, "The Figures Can Lie and Lies Can Figure When Poll Is Biased," *Chicago Tribune*, July 6, 1993, Perspective Section, p. 17.
8. Ken Schroeder, "Whose Hostile Hallways?" *Education Digest*, September 1993, p. 71.
9. Bonnie Erbe and Betsy Hart, "Harassment Study: Is It Vital or Misleading?" Pro/Con column, *South Bend Tribune*, June 6, 1993, p. 1.
10. Author E-mail correspondence with Shoop, May 7, 1994.

11. Ruth Z. Sweetser, "Sexual Harassment No Small Matter," *Chicago Tribune*, Perspective Section, p. 10.
12. SASH-L listserv posting, April 7, 1994 (poster requested anonymity).
13. Quoted in Lawrence Kutner, "Parent & Child" column, *The New York Times*, February 24, 1994, p. B5 (national edition).
14. Quoted in Linda Robertson (Knight-Ridder News Service), "Bond Delicate for Female Athlete, Male Coach," *Oregonian*, March 6, 1994, p. C14.
15. Quoted in David Foster (Associated Press), "Fear of Abuse Claims Making Adults Withhold Hugs," *South Bend Tribune*, March 20, 1994, p. A8.
16. Personal interview, Elkhart, Indiana, March 18, 1994.

Chapter Six

1. Quoted in Echo Montgomery Garrett, "What You Need to Know about Sexual Harassment [on college campuses]," *Money*, Winter 1994, p. 37.
2. Quoted in Eric Schmitt (New York Times News Service), "Air Force Responding to Harassment Charges," *South Bend Tribune*, May 1, 1994, p. A5.
3. Katie Roiphe, *The Morning After: Sex, Fear, and Feminism on Campus* (Boston: Little, Brown, 1993), p. 90.
4. Mary Matalin, "Stop Whining!" *Newsweek*, October 25, 1993, p. 62.
5. Judith Sherven, "Feminism Sells Women Short," Opinion Column, *Los Angeles Times*, March 2, 1994, p. B7.
6. Andi Ackerman, "Sherven on Feminism," Letter to the Editor, *Los Angeles Times*, March 10, 1994, p. B6.
7. Quoted in "New Rules about Sex on Campus" (Forum). *Harper's Magazine*, September 1993, p. 40.
8. Quoted in Deborah Taylor, SASH-L (listserv) electronic posting, April 13, 1994.
9. Pauline B. Bart, SASH-L (listserv) electronic posting, February 21, 1994.

10. Barry M. Dank, SASH-L (listserv) electronic posting, April 19, 1994.
11. Martin Schwartz, SASH-L (listserv) electronic posting, April 20, 1994.
12. "Syracuse Policy-D," SASH-L (listserv) electronic file, April 29, 1993.
13. Quoted in Vincent J. Schodolski, "Campus Quandary: Teacher-Student Love," *Chicago Tribune*, September 5, 1993, p. 21.
14. Quoted in "New Rules about Sex on Campus" (Forum), *Harper's Magazine*, September 1993, p. 36.
15. Barbara Beck, News and Public Affairs, University of Pennsylvania, news release, April 26, 1994.

Chapter Seven

1. Christina Hoff Sommers, "Capitol Hill's Girl Trouble," *The Washington Post*, July 17, 1994, Outlook Section, p. C1.
2. Congresswoman Patsy T. Mink, news release, April 21, 1993.
3. Barbara Kantrowitz, "Men, Women, Computers," *Newsweek*, May 16, 1994, p. 51.
4. Kimberly J. Cook, SASH-L (listserv) posting, February 18, 1994.
5. Quoted in Don Oldenburg, "Careerfile: When Girl Meets Computer," *The Washington Post*, March 24, 1993, p. B5.
6. James Knight, public lecture, Elkhart Area Career Center, Elkhart, Indiana, May 11, 1994.
7. Myra and David Sadker, "Why Schools Must Tell Girls: 'You're Smart, You Can Do It,' " *USA Weekend*, February 4–6, 1994, p. 5.
8. Ibid.

Chapter Eight

1. Anonymous remark overheard in an Indiana high school.

Selected Bibliography

American Association of University Women. *Hostile Hallways: The AAUW Survey on Sexual Harassment in America's Schools*. Washington, D.C.: American Association of University Women, 1993.

American Association of University Women. *How Schools Shortchange Girls: A Study of Major Findings on Girls and Education*. Washington, D.C.: American Association of University Women, 1991.

Atkins, Andrea. "Sexual Harassment in School: Is Your Child at Risk?" *Better Homes and Gardens*, August 1992, pp. 32–34.

Auster, Bruce B. "The Navy Sets a Different Course." *U.S. News & World Report*, May 3, 1993, pp. 49–50.

Barlow, Dudley. "The Right Never to Be Uncomfortable?" *Education Digest*, February 1994, pp. 13–16.

Begley, Sharon, with Pat Wingert, Farai Chideya, Jenny Duffy, Debra Rosenberg, and Dogen Hannah. "Hands Off, Mr. Chips!" *Newsweek*, May 3, 1993, p. 58.

Bouchard, Elizabeth. *Everything You Need to Know about Sexual Harassment*. New York: The Rosen Publishing Group, Inc., 1992.

Boxall, Bettina; Greg Krikorian; and Jim Newton. "Sexual Harassment a Tough LAPD Problem." *Los Angeles Times,* March 3, 1994, p. A1.

Branah, Karen. "Out for Blood: The Right's Vendetta Against Anita Hill's Supporters." *Ms.* January/February 1994, pp. 82–87.

Bravo, Ellen, and Ellen Cassedy. "Is It Sexual Harassment?" *Redbook,* July 1992, pp. 53–56.

Bravo, Ellen, and Ellen Cassedy. *The 9to5 Guide to Combating Sexual Harassment.* New York: Wiley, 1992.

Charney, Dara A., and Ruth C. Russell. "An Overview of Sexual Harassment." *American Journal of Psychiatry,* January 1994, pp. 10–17.

Crichton, Sarah. "Sexual Correctness: Has It Gone Too Far?" *Newsweek,* October 25, 1993, pp. 52–58.

Dworkin, Terry Morehead. "Harassment in the 1990s." *Business Horizons,* March/April 1993, pp. 52–58.

Eskenazi, Martin, and David Gallen. *Sexual Harassment: Know Your Rights!* New York: Carroll & Graf, 1992.

Fisher, Anne B. "Sexual Harassment: What to Do." *Fortune,* August 23, 1993, pp. 84–88.

Francke, Linda Bird. "Paula Coughlin: The Woman Who Changed the U.S. Navy." *Glamour,* June 1993, pp. 158–161, 216–220.

Gleick, Elizabeth, and Margaret Nelson. "The Boys on the Bus." *People,* November 30, 1992, pp. 125–126.

Greve, Michael S., and Linda Hirshman. "First Amendment: Do 'Hostile Environment' Charges Chill Academic Freedom?" *ABA Journal,* February 1994, pp. 40–41.

Hales, Dianne, and Dr. Robert Hales. "Can Men and Women Work Together?" *Parade,* March 20, 1994, pp. 10–11.

Hentoff, Nat. "Sexual Harassment by Francisco Goya." *The Washington Post,* December 27, 1991, p. A21.

Hill, Anita. "No Regrets." *Essence,* March 1992, pp. 55–56, 116, 119.

Hodgson, Harriet W. *Powerplays: How Teens Can Pull the Plug on Sexual Harassment.* Minneapolis: Deaconess Press, 1993.

Jacobbi, Marianne. " 'Just Call Me Doctor.' " *Good Housekeeping*, August 1992, pp. 64–68.

Jacobbi, Marianne. " 'Why I Had to Speak Out About Tailhook.' " *Good Housekeeping*, June 1993, pp. 95, 158–160.

Jordan, Mary. "Case of He Said, She Said Embroils Swarthmore in 'Sexual Politics.' " *The Washington Post*, January 27, 1994, p. A3.

Kadetsky, Elizabeth. "The Million-Dollar Man." *Working Woman*, October 1993, pp. 46–49, 78–79.

Kantrowitz, Barbara, with Pat Wingert and Patrick Houston. "Sexism in the Schoolhouse." *Newsweek*, February 24, 1992, p. 62.

Kaplan, David A. "Take Down the Girlie Calendars." *Newsweek*, November 22, 1993, p. 34.

Kaplan, Joel, and David Aronson. "The Numbers Gap." *Teaching Tolerance*, Spring 1994, pp. 21–27.

Kaus, Mickey. "Street Hassle." *New Republic*, March 22, 1993, pp. 4–5.

Kennelly, Jim. "The Big Chill at School." *USA Weekend*, January 14–16, 1994, p. 18.

Kipnis, Aaron, and Elizabeth Herron. *Gender War, Gender Peace: The Quest for Love and Justice Between Women and Men*. New York: Morrow, 1994.

Kuster, Elizabeth. "Don't 'Hey, Baby' Me." *Glamour*, September 1992, pp. 309–311, 332–333.

Kutner, Lawrence. "With a 1990's Awareness of Sexual Harassment, Grownups Look at 'Harmless' School Bus Teasing." *The New York Times* (national edition), February 24, 1994, p. B5.

Landau, Elaine. *Sexual Harassment*. New York: Walker, 1993.

Langelan, Martha J. *Back Off! How to Confront and Stop Sexual Harassment and Harassers*. New York: Simon and Schuster, 1993.

LeBlanc, Adrian Nicole. "Harassment at School: The Truth Is Out." *Seventeen*, May 1993, pp. 134–135.

Mason, Deborah. "The Pain of Sexual Harassment After 50." *New Choices*, September 1993, pp. 16–21.

McCann, Nancy Dodd, and Thomas A. McGinn. *Harassed: 100 Women Define Inappropriate Behavior in the Workplace.* Homewood, Ill.: Business One Irwin, 1992.

McKay, Mike, and Barrie Beth Hansen. "Should You Ever Touch a Student?" (Debate). *NEA Today,* February 1994, p. 39.

Monagle, Katie. " 'You Just Don't Get It.' " *Scholastic Update,* March 12, 1993, pp. 2–5.

Morris, Barbra, with Jacquie Terpstra, Bob Croninger, and Eleanor Linn. *Tune in to Your Rights: A Guide for Teenagers about Turning Off Sexual Harassment.* Ann Arbor: Center for Sex Equity in Schools, University of Michigan, 1985.

Morris, Celia. *Bearing Witness: Sexual Harassment and Beyond—Everywoman's Story.* Boston and London: Little, Brown, 1994.

Mullery, Virginia. "It's Chemistry: For Years, Girls and Science Didn't Mix." *Chicago Tribune,* September 5, 1993, Section 18, p. 3.

"New Rules About Sex on Campus" (Forum). *Harper's Magazine,* September 1993, pp. 33–42.

Noble, Linda. "My Struggle to Fight Harassment." *Glamour,* May 1994, p. 139.

Paludi, Michele, ed. *Ivory Power: Sexual Harassment on Campus.* Albany, N.Y.: State University of New York Press, 1990.

Petrocelli, William, and Barbara Kate Repa. *Sexual Harassment on the Job.* Berkeley, Calif.: Nolo Press, 1992.

Phillips, Susan P., and Margaret S. Schneider. "Sexual Harassment of Female Doctors by Patients." *New England Journal of Medicine,* December 23, 1993, pp. 1936–1939.

Pollan, Stephen M., and Mark Levine. "Confronting a Sexual Harasser. Finding the Right Words." *Working Woman,* March 1994, p. 71.

"A Professor's Suspension Prompts Debate Over Campus Free Speech." *The New York Times* (national edition), February 27, 1994, p. 13.

Reed, Julia. "The Burden of Proof." *Vogue,* January 1994, pp. 32–33.

Roiphe, Katie. *The Morning After: Sex, Fear, and Feminism on Campus*. Boston and London: Little, Brown, 1993.

Sadker, Myra and David. "Fair and Square: Creating a Nonsexist Classroom." *Instructor*, March 1993, pp. 44–46, 67–68.

Saltzman, Amy. "It's Not Just Teasing." *U.S. News & World Report*, December 6, 1993, pp. 73–77.

Sandroff, Ronni. "Sexual Harassment." *Working Woman*, June 1992, pp. 47–51, 78.

Seal, Kathy. "Sexual Harassment in Our Schools." *First for Women*, February 14, 1994, pp. 92–93.

Segal, Troy, with Kevin Kelly and Alisa Solomon. "Getting Serious about Sexual Harassment." *Business Week*, November 9, 1992, pp. 78, 82.

"Sexual Harassment: Is There a Feminist Double Standard?" *Ms.*, March/April 1993, p. 89.

Shalit, Ruth. "Romper Room: Sexual Harassment—by Tots." *New Republic*, March 29, 1993, pp. 13–15.

Shoop, Robert J., and Jack W. Hayhow, Jr. *Sexual Harassment in Our Schools: What Parents and Teachers Need to Know to Spot It and Stop It!* Boston: Allyn & Bacon, 1994.

Shroeder, Ken. "Whose Hostile Hallways?" *Education Digest*, September 1993, pp. 71–72.

Siegel, Deborah L. *Sexual Harassment: Research & Resources*. New York: National Council for Research on Women, 1992.

Smith, Max. "Down These Mean Streets." *Essence*, May 1993, p. 152.

Smith, Wes. "Trial and Error? Did a University Go Too Far in Getting Tough on Date Rape?" *Chicago Tribune Magazine*, May 1, 1994, pp. 15–23.

Sommers, Christina Hoff. "Capital Hill's Girl Trouble: The Flawed Study Behind the Gender Equity Act." *The Washington Post*, July 17, 1994, p. C1.

Spaid, Elizabeth Levitan. "Schools Grapple with Peer Harassment." *Christian Science Monitor*, January 21, 1993, p. 3.

Starr, Tama. "A Reasonable Woman." *Reason*, February 1994, pp. 48–49.

Stein, Nan. "Stop Sexual Harassment in Schools." *USA Today*, May 18, 1993, p. 11A.

Stein, Nan; Nancy L. Marshall; and Linda R. Tropp. *Secrets in Public: Sexual Harassment in Our Schools*. Wellesley, Mass.: Center for Research on Women, Wellesley College, 1993.

Stephson, Amy. *Sexual Harassment in Employment and Education*. Seattle: Northwest Women's Law Center, 1992.

Strauss, Susan, with Pamela Espeland. *Sexual Harassment and Teens*. Minneapolis: Free Spirit Publishing, 1992.

Swisher, Kara. "Laying Down the Law on Harassment." *The Washington Post*, February 6, 1994, p. H1.

Tunick, George. "When the Tables Are Turned." *Executive Female*, March/April 1994, p. 78.

Vachss, Alice. *Sex Crimes*. New York: Random House, 1993.

Walker, Michael. "Gender Bias." *Better Homes and Gardens*, April 1993, pp. 40–42.

Webb, Susan L. *Step Forward: Sexual Harassment in the Workplace: What You Need to Know*. New York: MasterMedia, 1992.

Woodward, Kenneth L., and Stanley Holmes. "Sexual or Textual Harassment?" *Newsweek*, May 9, 1994, pp. 56–57.

Young, Cathy. "Is It Mischief or Sexual Harassment?" *Chicago Tribune*, June 22, 1993, Perspective Section, p. 19.

Resources

African American Women in Defense of Ourselves, 317 South Division, Suite 199, Ann Arbor, MI 48104

American Association of University Women Legal Advocacy Fund, 1111 16th Street NW, Washington, DC 20036

American Civil Liberties Union, 132 West 43rd Street, New York, NY 10036

American Federation of Teachers, Human Rights Department, 555 New Jersey Avenue NW, Washington, DC 20001

Bureau of National Affairs Communications, 9439 Key West Avenue, Rockville, MD 20850

Center for Women and Policy Studies, 2000 P Street NW, Suite 508, Washington, DC 20036

Center for Women in Government, State University of New York at Albany, Draper Hall, Room 310, Albany, NY 12222

Center for Working Life, 600 Grand Avenue, Suite 305, Oakland, CA 94610

Coalition on Sexual Harassment, c/o New York Women's Foundation, 120 Wooster Street, New York, NY 10012

Equal Employment Opportunity Commission, 1801 L Street NW, Washington, DC 20507

Federation of Organizations for Professional Women, 2001 S Street NW, Suite 500, Washington, DC 20009

Fund for the Feminist Majority, 1600 Wilson Boulevard, Suite 704, Arlington, VA 22209

National Coalition Against Sexual Assault, Box 21378, Washington, DC 20009

National Council for Research on Women, Sexual Harassment Information Project, 47–49 East 65th Street, New York, NY 10021

National Education Association, Human and Civil Rights Department, 1201 16th Street NW, Washington, DC 20036

National Women's Law Center, 1616 P Street NW, Washington, DC 20036

National Women's Political Caucus, 1275 K Street NW, Suite 750, Washington, DC 20005

9to5, National Association of Working Women, 614 Superior Avenue NW, Cleveland, OH 44113

Northwest Women's Law Center, 119 South Main Street, Suite 330, Seattle, WA 98104

NOW Legal Defense and Education Fund, 99 Hudson Street, New York, NY 10013

Women's Alliance for Job Equity, 1422 Chestnut Street, Suite 1100, Philadelphia, PA 19102

Women's Bureau, U.S. Department of Labor, Washington, DC 20210

Women's Legal Defense Fund, 1875 Connecticut Avenue NW, Suite 710, Washington, DC 20009

Index

Abbott Laboratories, 99
Abelard, Peter, 86
Ackerman, Andi, 85
Adams, John, 38
African Americans, 30–31, 98
Air Force Academy, Colorado
  Springs, 82
Allred, Gloria, 19
American Association for the
  Advancement of Science
  (AAAS), 99
American Association of
  University Women
  (AAUW), 25, 69–70, 96–
  98, 100
Anderson, Cordelia, 76
Antioch College, 83

Baigrie, Brian, 63
Brawdy, Tawyna, 66–67
Brock, David, 32

Campus, sexual harassment
  on, 15, 79–93
Center for Sex Equity in
  Schools, University of
  Michigan, 75–76
Chicago Theological
  Seminary, 80–81
Civil Rights Act of 1964, 20,
  21, 25, 27
  1991 amendments to (Title
  VII), 27, 64
Clay, William L., 61
Clinansmith, Alexis, 81–82
Computer Expert Equity
  Project (CEEP), 100, 101
Congressional Caucus for
  Women's Issues, 98
Conley, Frances, 11, 55–56
Consenting Academics for
  Sexual Equality (CASE),
  88–90